"Gertie McDowell belongs in the top list of first-person narrators along with Huck Finn and Holden Caulfield ... So congratulations author Hanna. You gave us more laughs than a bucketful of minnows."

> – Jon Michael Miller, Readers' Favorite Awards

"The Ping-Pong Champion of Chinatown is wildly entertaining. In fact, I read it in one sitting. Gertie's southern hick charm comes right across in James Hanna's writing as if she were sitting right next to you telling you her story."

> – Kristi Elizabeth, Manhattan Book Reviews

"Gertie is very relatable; she is organic, has a distinct personality, and her accounts are captivating... This book is hilareous and, more often than not, I couldn't help chuckling."

> – Online Book Club

"If you ever watched the movies Calamity Jane or Annie Get Your Gun, two of my all-time favorites, you'll know that Gertie belongs up on the big screen with them. What a character!"

> – Viga Boland, Readers' Favorite Awards

"I adored the expressive metaphors, such as 'I was dumber than broccoli' or 'My heart hopped like a duck on a Junebug'."

> – Online Book Club

Other books by James Hanna

The Siege: A Prison Uprising Redefines Justice

Call Me Pomeroy: A Novel of Satire and Political Dissent

A Second, Less Capable, Head: And Other Rogue Stories

Shackles and More Gripping Tales

Awards received by James Hanna...

 The 2017 Readers' Favorite International Awards gave James Hanna's novel, *Call Me Pomeroy*, the gold medal in the humor category.

 The 2017 Readers' Favorite International Awards gave James Hanna's novel, *The Siege*, the bronze medal in the literary fiction category.

 The 2017 Independent Press Awards gave James Hanna's short story collection, *A Second, Less Capable Head and Other Rogue Stories*, a silver medal in the anthology category.

 The 2018 Readers' Favorite International Awards gave James Hanna's short story collection, *A Second, Less Capable Head and Other Rogue Stories*, the gold medal in the anthology category.

The Ping-Pong Champion of Chinatown

By

James Hanna

The Ping-Pong Champion of Chinatown

By
James Hanna

Published by Sand Hill Review Press www.sandhillreviewpress.com,
1 Baldwin Ave, #304, San Mateo, CA 94401
(415) 297-3571

Library of Congress Control Number: 2010920295

ISBN: 978-1-949534-18-4 (paperback)
ISBN: 978-1-949534-26-9 (ebook)

Art Direction by Tory Hartmann, Sand Hill Review Press
Graphics by Backspace Ink

CIP Data Block
Names: Hanna, James, author.
Title: The ping-pong champion of Chinatown / by James Hanna.
Description: San Mateo, CA: Sand Hill Review Press, 2021.
Identifiers: LCCN: 2010920295 | ISBN: 978-1-949534-18-4 (paperback) |
978-1-949534-26-9 (ebook)
Subjects: LCSH Witness protection programs--Fiction. | Fetishism (Sexual
behavior)--Fiction. | Dressmaking--Fiction. | Drug traffic--Fiction. |
Texas--Fiction. | Table tennis--Fiction. | United States. Federal industrial
institution for women, Alderson, W.Va.--Fiction. | Female offenders-
-United States--Fiction. | United States--California--San Francisco-
-Fiction. | Diaries--Fiction. | Humorous stories. | BISAC FICTION /
General | FICTION / Humorous / General
Classification: LCC PS3608.A26 P56 2021 | DDC 813.6--dc23

SHRP
Sand Hill Review Press
1 BALDWIN AVE, #304, SAN MATEO, CA 94401

To Antaeus, Teri, and Glenna

"Give a girl the right shoes, and she can conquer the world."

Marilyn Monroe

Contents

Foreword

WELCOME TO *The Ping-Pong Champion of Chinatown*! You're about to enter the madcap world of twenty-three-year-old Gertie McDowell from Turkey Roost, Kentucky. Gertie's desire to escape from a town that's "just a whole lot of nothing" leads her from one misadventure to another. In addition to inadvertently muling powdered meth, becoming a "video star," a "famous dress designer," a ping-pong champion, Gertie is kidnapped into white slavery, makes an outfit for a prison warden, rides a fetish float in the San Francisco Gay Pride Parade, and becomes a mechanical bull riding hustler in Texas.

The eight interconnected stories with peculiar titles like "Crossing the Jordan" and "Armadillo Slick," are filled with wry humor, sometimes the result of the narrator, sometimes the characters' own particular idiom. But Hanna's writing also complicates the lives of "a good-hearted girl who keeps getting led astray" and the men and women she encounters who, for all their big-dreaming, bravado, and momentary successes, will never ultimately beat the system. We simultaneously root for Gertie while always anticipating her downfall.

Not only are the stories comical, but they're linguistically skillful and quirky. Gertie possesses a hilarious manner of expression, particularly in her penchant for likening people or events to animals. A man grabs her hand "like a pigeon snatchin' a fry"; a waitress is described as slipping out of a customer's grip like "a lizard shedding its tail"; one man is said to be "skinnier than an otter"; a car glides alongside Gertie like "a vulture fixing to land." Since each story is told from Gertie's point of view, the "Gertie-isms" never let up.

And the wordplay doesn't stop with Gertie's bizarre analogies. Most of the characters are given or take on pseudonyms, such as "the Nose" of "Foothold Agency," so named because he sniffs shoes and makes foot fetish videos. Many characters adopt literary names as disguises. A meth dealer calls himself "Jean Valjean" from Victor Hugo's novel *Les Misérables,* another is "Sancho Panza" from Cervantes' *Don Quixote.* Some names are just droll, such as "Warden Jordan" in the prison where Gertie is briefly an inmate. Gertie McDowell herself, unbeknown to her, is derived from Gertie McDowell, a parodic construction of stereotypes, from James Joyce's *Ulysses.*

Hanna treats his Gertie with more fondness and sympathy than Joyce, however, allowing her to genuinely grow and even become "philosophical." As the stories develop, Gertie amusingly speculates about events in the Bible such as how Cain managed to have that son in the Land of Nod, finds love, and gives up her need for a guardian angel, reflecting that "them angels have gotta be blinder than moles and without the sense God gave a turnip." Perhaps most generously, Hanna ultimately allows Gertie to stop seeking the elusive fame that always leads to disappointment: "Shucks, a cool glass of lemonade on a front porch is a whole lot better than fame."

Hanna's stories both fully incorporate their locale, drawing his readers in and getting us to sympathize with and thoroughly enjoy Gertie and his colorful cast of secondary characters—and also transcend it to gently critique the system that keeps certain types of people small. This combination, to me, is the core and cleverness of Hanna's writing.

—Kathleen McCormick, Prof. of Literature & Writing, SUNY Purchase, author of *Dodging Satan: My Irish/Italian Sometimes Awesome, But Mostly Creepy Childhood* (SHRP, 2016)

Preface

IF YOU'RE READING THIS BOOK, I'm gonna consider you a friend. It ain't like you gotta meet me 'cause I'm kind of a bad influence, but if you keep me at a distance, you could probably be my friend. A girl can't have too many friends even if she's gotta make 'em up.

Anyhow, my name is Gertie McDowell, I'm twenty-three years old and I've scribbled me this here journal. I've been scribbling it since I was an eighteen-year-old stuck in Turkey Roost, Kentucky. I was born in Turkey Roost, but I don't stay there no more. I'm livin' in South Texas now, which ain't a whole lot better, but at least I can ride the mechanical bulls in some of them honky-tonk bars. I'm real good at riding them robot bulls, and I'm good at other stuff too. I was an internet star on a fetish site, but I don't do that no more. I was also a famous dress designer, but I hadda quit that too. I was even an undercover agent way out in San Francisco—that's 'cause this detective asked me to infiltrate a white slavery ring. On top of that, I was the best checker player in all of Alderson Prison—that's a women's facility in West Virginia where Martha Stewart once stayed. I done time there 'cause I got into some trouble, which was kinda accidental. But what I'm best at is ping-pong—I won me a championship. That happened while I was living in San Francisco's Chinatown. I was hiding out in Chinatown under the Witness Protection Program, so I guess it weren't too smart of me to become no ping-pong champion. But I won a gold-colored trophy and a coupon for the Golden Gate

3

Bakery—them prizes weren't nothing special but they made me feel proud as a lord.

I ain't too good at arranging a book, but James Hanna he helped me with that. I met James Hanna in Cherokee Sal's, a honky-tonk in Laredo where I ride the mechanical bull. He was eating a buffalo burger with fries and drinking a bottle of stout, and he was reading this book in Latin that's called *The Iliad*. I figgered anyone reading a book in Latin was a writing kind of fella, so I asked him if he wouldn't mind making my book presentable. James Hanna said he would be glad to help 'cause he needed a writing project, so while he finished his buffalo burger, I went home and fetched him my journal.

Now James Hanna he's known for stretchin' the truth so's to have him a colorful yarn. But my stories don't need no stretchin 'cause they're crazy enough as it is. I wrote 'em down while they was happening and I ain't corrected 'em much, but whether folks like my grammar or not, I hope they read this book. Shucks, I don't wanna pass out of this world without leavin' no mark upon it, and I figger these stories are more 'an sufficient to let folks know I been here. So I wanna thank James Hanna for helping me with this book. 'Cause he cleaned up my spelling and grammar a tad and presented them stories good.

1. Little Miss Twinkle Toes

LIKE I SAID, my name is Gertie McDowell. And I was born in Turkey Roost, which ain't much to brag about. The town, if you want to call it that, has half a dozen streets, a whole bunch of bars and a McDonald's whose arches are always powdered with coal dust. Just a typical strip-mining town is all. On Saturday night, a girl can't do much except stroll up and down the main drag. Or maybe fix herself some popcorn and watch movies on the Turner channel. I watch a lot of movies, and I like old musicals best. My favorite is *West Side Story*—Natalie Wood sure could sing. But I'm kinda getting off the subject.

Most girls marry young in Turkey Roost—that's just the way it is. A lot of them are mothers at sixteen—grandmothers when they reach their thirties. Folks got a saying in Turkey Roost if ya don't want to hang around. "You got three choices here," they say. "Coal mine, moonshine, or see you on down the line." I chose *see you on down the line*, but it didn't work out too well.

I don't want to talk no more about Turkey Roost—the town is just a whole lot of nothing. What I want to tell you about is this crazy summer I spent in Los Angeles. I went there to become a movie star because I have singing and acting talent. I played the lead in *Annie* when I was only a junior in high school. I got a

5

standing ovation too. Everyone in the school auditorium, all fifty people, were on their feet pounding their palms when I took the curtain call.

People tell me I'm the prettiest girl that Turkey Roost ever sprouted. I think they might be exaggerating a tad—my bust is just thirty-one inches. So when I went to a photographer in Nashville to get some glossies made, I wore a padded bra that I stuffed with tissue paper. I also tucked in my chin like Lauren Bacall did in *To Have and Have Not*. That made me look so sexy the photographer gave me a discount. He took three glossies of me and charged me just five hundred dollars.

After graduating from high school—I was eighth in a class of thirteen—I sent my glossies and acting resumé to all the big studios in Hollywood. When I didn't get an answer from them, I took destiny by the horns. I dyed my hair strawberry blonde, I bought a one-way Greyhound ticket to Los Angeles, and I said goodbye to everyone who watched me perform in *Annie*. Most of them said I would soon be a star because I remembered almost all my lines. They asked me to remember *them* when I was starring opposite Brad Pitt.

*

WHEN I GOT TO LOS ANGELES, I rented a room in a Super 8 Motel in Koreatown. It's a pretty cool place with a kidney-shaped swimming pool and fifty cable channels. And I got a part-time job at Wendy's—twenty hours a week. That left me enough time to beat the pavement and land a movie role.

Well, I went to a lot of agencies and gave them my glossies and resumé. But none of them wanted to make me a star. They said I needed more experience, they said I needed a theatrical degree, they said I needed to become a member of the Screen Actors Guild. And when I went to a couple of casting calls, that didn't go well either. The directors said they wouldn't audition me until I had an agent.

Well, to cheer myself up, I went to the Walk of Fame on Hollywood Boulevard. It was neat to see the stars' names on the sidewalk, but the street was pretty dirty. It was also full of homeless folks, pickpockets, and pushy hawkers wearing movie star costumes. When this girl dressed like Shirley Temple tried to snatch my purse, I hopped onto a metro bus and returned to Koreatown.

But the *really* weird stuff didn't happen to me until I'd been in Los Angeles a month. I was sitting on the grass in Griffith Park, sipping a diet cola, and I kicked off my Birkenstock sandals because my feet were kinda sore. That's when I saw this middle-aged gentleman filming me with a cell phone. He was skinnier than an otter and he had this little goat beard, and he was wearing these mirrored sunglasses that spat the sun into my eyes. He wasn't even trying to *hide* the fact that he was filming me. He just stood on the park path, cool as a snow cone, and pointed his cell phone at me.

"Whatcha doin', mister?" I asked him.

The dude tucked his phone into his shirt pocket and grinned like a grape eatin' possum. Then he opened up his wallet and handed me a business card. The card said *The Nose, Foothold Agency, 200 South San Pedro Street.* It had a picture of a stiletto shoe and website and Facebook links.

"You a talent scout, Mister?" I said because I was feeling kind of flattered.

"A talent scout?!" he said—his voice was so warm and syrupy it coulda been poured over waffles. "Why do you ask, little missy? Did you star in some high school production?"

"Yeah," I said in my huskiest tone, and I turned my good side toward him. "I got a standing ovation too."

The dude looked at me kinda funny then he snorted like a stallion. "Standing ovations—pah!" he said. "They're as common as pepper and salt."

"Well, I got as much talent as Wendy has burgers," I said, and I straightened my dress.

"Do you?" he said. The dude bowed his head as though he was at a funeral. He musta been an outta work actor who needed himself a stage. "In that case, I weep for you, little missy," he said. "You will soon be hamburger too."

"Whatcha mean by that?" I said.

The dude he started talking to me like he was livin' in a play. "'As much talent as Wendy has burgers'," he repeated. "What a gullible thing to say. Wendy isn't real, you know—she's crimson-haired will-'o-the-wisp. Her siren song will lure you to fall upon barnacled rocks."

I wasn't quite sure what he meant by that—I ain't good with fancy talk. So I said to him, "I seen *Ghost Busters* six or seven times."

I guess I shouldn't have started no chat with a dude that weren't right in the head. Especially, when he was staring at me like *I* was the crazy one. "So how come you're filmin' me, mister?" I said.

Well, he grabbed my hand and shook it like a pigeon snatchin' a fry. "Call it a fated attraction," he said, "or the noble heart of Ulysses. I leap to the rescue of damsels as though summoned by Circe's spell."

Dern, if that wasn't a gobful, and I guess I shoulda been impressed. But Ulysses looks like George Clooney—I seen him in *Oh Brother Where Art Thou?* So I said to the dude, "You ain't Ulysses" 'cause I didn't want him to think I was dumb.

Well, he puffed out his chest like a banty rooster then pressed my hand to his heart. "And yet *you* are my Penelope," he said. "My golden-haired Ithaca queen."

"If ya wanna be my agent," I said, "ya don't gotta act all mushy."

He slapped his chest as though wounded—I guess I insulted him. "Your agent?" he said. "I will be more than that. I will beat off false suitors, safeguard your virtue, empower you to walk among stars. If you need a guardian angel, miss, you need look no further than me."

Dern, if I didn't start liking the fella in spite of his crazy talk. Or maybe I felt kinda sorry for him 'cause he reminded me of a stray dog. When I was a girl, I was all the time bringing home dogs that were on the loose. Beagles, terriers, mongrels—you name it— they was all the time following me home. Ma said it was like I had a pork chop tied 'round my neck. So I didn't make no objection when the dude kept on filming me. I just posed like I was Penelope Cruz and wiggled my toes in the grass.

*

THE MAN TOLD ME to come to his studio apartment at 200 South San Pedro Street. He wrote out some directions and said to meet him there the next day. He even kissed my hand, like Maurice Chevalier mighta done, and said that deep in his heart a candle burned for me. Well, I ain't quite sure what he had in mind, but I suppose he was planning a screen test. After all, he had promised me that I was gonna walk among stars.

When I got off the metro at South San Pedro Street, I didn't feel particularly impressed. The neighborhood was full of homeless camps, tattoo parlors and gated houses. There were gangs of boys in hoodies lurking in front of warehouses, and folks were making drug deals all up and down the street. And whenever a cop car cruised by—which happened 'bout every five minutes— some of them people made police siren noises and shouted out, "Five-Oh!"

When I found out where that fella lived, I was tempted to walk away. He lived in some tiny hovel beside a porno shop. But I pressed the buzzer on the door 'cause I wanted to get off the street, and I recognized his voice when it came on the intercom.

"*Keep your eyes on the stars, your feet on the ground,*" he said in this garbled tone. I guess he was maybe quotin' someone, but I ain't sure who it was. All I knew is my feet had blisters, and I wanted to give them a soak.

I spoke my name into the intercom, and he said, "*Come in, my child.*" The door lock popped open like a chestnut exploding on a hearth.

Well, I pushed my way into the building and I ran a comb through my hair, and I walked up this flight of stairs so narrow it felt like I was wearing a girdle. His apartment was cluttered and dirty and smelled kinda like dirty socks. There weren't much furniture in it neither—just a couch and a dining room set—and this creepy movie camera on stilts was propped up next to the window.

The dude he was sitting at the table, still wearing them mirrored sunglasses, and he was sniffing a woman's stiletto and watching a monitor. Well, I decided right then and there that I was gonna get out of that place. But before I could walk back down the stairs, the dude whipped out a checkbook.

"Shoot for the moon, little missy," he shouted. "If you miss you will land among stars." And he wrote me a check for five hundred dollars and slapped it into the palm of my hand.

"What's this for?" I asked him.

"It's a tribute," he said. "Alms to a waif who will soon shine as bright as Polaris. Just like Eliza Doolittle, you will soar to celestial heights."

I think he was talking 'bout *My Fair Lady*—I saw that on the Turner channel once. But it still didn't make no sense to me, so I handed him back the check.

"Do little?" I said. "I done nothing for this."

"Au contraire, little cherub," he said, and he shoved the check back in my hand. "Does the Mona Lisa do nothing? Does Diana the Huntress do nothing? Does Botticelli's Venus do nothing as she rises from the sea? These are not still-life paintings, my dear, but angels arrested in flight. The mere image of such goddesses amounts to a symphony."

Well, I ain't never heard no symphony, but I seen David Bowie on YouTube. 'Cept he called himself Ziggy Stardust, and his band was called The Spiders from Mars. When I told the dude about this, he gave me a smooch on the forehead. "Consider it a premonition," he said. "A portent of starlight to come."

The dude went to this tiny refrigerator and came back with a bottle of champagne. And he poured us each a glass, and we toasted to my future success. Then he typed some stuff on a keyboard, and this website popped up on the monitor. And he kissed his fingers just like a Frenchman and shouted, "Venus arise!"

Well, I saw myself on the website, and I didn't look like no goddess. I was slurpin' a diet cola and wiggling my toes in the grass. But it weren't the video that made me feel like I'd come to Crazytown. It was the logo he put on the website—the looniest thing I seen. It seemed that I was gonna be known as Little Miss Twinkle Toes.

*

THE NOSE—that's what I'm gonna call the dude since I seen him sniffing that shoe—the Nose told me I had over a hundred subscribers, and they were paying ten dollars a month. He had also prepared me a Facebook page, and he said I had lots of friend requests. When I asked him if posing shoeless was going to make me a movie star, he said Meryl Streep, Audrey Hepburn and Charo

11

all got their start the same way. The trick, he said, was to engage with my fans and to offer 'em new stuff each day.

So every day for a month, I went to his pad and he made a video of my feet. I stood barefoot on sheets of bubble wrap and popped them under my heels. I stood up to my ankles in strawberry Jell-O and sprayed Reddi-wip on my soles. I even stood in a tub of nightcrawlers—worms you use for fishing—and I waved a fishing pole around while I picked up the worms with my toes.

Eventually, the Nose gave me some sparkly nail polish—he said I needed a trademark look. When I painted it on my toenails, they glittered just like opals. He also made me go to a doctor to get a wart on my big toe removed. I gotta admit that smarted—the doc used an electric needle. But you have to suffer a little if you're gonna become a star. So I gritted my teeth like Katharine Hepburn and didn't complain at all.

By the end of the month, that website had over two thousand subscribers. And I spent hours each day on my Facebook page answering questions from fans. A lot of them wanted to buy my shoes, but I only had one pair of sandals. So the Nose bought fifty pairs of stilettos—he got a deal on Craigslist—and he had me carve my initials on 'em then he sold 'em to my fans.

Well, soon I had more money than Kentucky has lumps of coal. So I quit my job at Wendy's and moved into Beverly Hills Hilton. And I rented a limousine every night to take me to a fancy restaurant. I always ordered pork chops 'cause they made me think of home, and I always gave the waiter a fifty-dollar tip.

The money kept piling up on me no matter how much I spent. The Nose said my incomparable talent had made me a household name. So I went to Rothstein Jewelers and bought a pair of diamond-studded sunglasses. They glittered as bright as my toenails, and they made me feel like Elizabeth Taylor. And I wore them whenever I was out in the sun 'cause that's what big stars do.

*

THAT WEBSITE SOON PICKED UP four thousand subscribers, but no movie offers came in. So the Nose he kept making videos of my feet to get me more exposure. He filmed me standing in a vat of mashed potatoes, pouring gravy onto my arches. He filmed me putting mustard on my toes then wrappin' them sideways in hotdog buns. He also filmed me wearing Valentino stilettos and stomping on balloons. But I didn't hear from no studios except for one called Caballero Productions. They wanted me to star in a remake of *Seven Brides for Seven Brothers*. 'Cept they were gonna call it *One Bride for Seven Brothers*. Well, I turned 'em down flat 'cause I don't think that movie would play well in Turkey Roost.

Well, another month passed and no offers came in, and my toes started getting chapped. So I told the Nose I wanted to take a vacation and soak my feet in milk. The Nose told me there weren't no time for that 'cause I had too busy a schedule. He said he'd booked me to do a commercial for Dr. Scholl's Corn Remover. He told me my fans had nominated me for the Shiniest Arches Award, and I had to attend this awards celebration that was gonna be held in Palmdale. He also told me this politician, some fellow running for the state senate, wanted me to pay him a visit at his home in Beverly Hills. The guy wanted me to step in peanut butter then walk all over his back.

Well, I ain't quite sure what got into me—guess I lost my feel for my fans. Or maybe I got temperamental like Joan Crawford and Lindsay Lohan. 'Cause when the Nose told me to wax my arches, I got as mean as a snake. I bought me a pair of combat boots and I laced them up past my ankles, and when he asked me to take them off, I told him the knots were too tight.

The Nose said I had a divine obligation to share my gift with the world. He said he'd commissioned a portrait of me that would be on a postage stamp, and he said he could smell a star for me on The Hollywood Walk of Fame. Well, I thanked the Nose for making me famous, and I gave him a kiss on the cheek. And I told him them big ol' combat boots were staying on my feet.

*

WELL, I'M BACK TO LIVING IN Turkey Roost now, and I got a job at the Walmart in Bowling Green, and I still watch the movie classics when they come on the Turner channel. Turkey Roost is still a whole lot of nothing, and that kinda bothers me. But a whole lot of nothing beats going to Palmdale to receive some pervert award.

The Nose he phoned me the other day—I ain't blocked my cell phone yet. He said he bought me a new pair of slingbacks 'cause my fans were begging for me. He said he lives in darkness now—his candle don't burn no more—and he asked me to pose for more videos so he could once again bathe in the light.

Well, I told the Nose he could send back them shoes, and I hope he kept the receipt. I told him my feet were retired and to find another star.

2. The Sugar Shack Dress Company

HI, IT'S GERTIE MCDOWELL AGAIN. You probably remember what happened to me when I went to Los Angeles to become a movie star. You probably recall how this gentleman—a dude who calls himself the Nose—took videos of my feet and put them on an internet website. Maybe you've even seen the videos—the site has a whole lot of subscribers. The Nose says one of them videos—the one where I'm picking up worms with my toes—had twenty thousand hits.

I still keep in touch with the Nose, you know? Yeah, he's kind of a pervert, but he ain't too bad a guy otherwise, and I like to hear him talk. Only the Nose could say things like "Keep your eyes on the stars and your feet on the ground." So whenever I'm lonely for intelligent conversation—which is just about all the time—I call the Nose on my cell phone and we have a little chat. 'Course, he begs me to come back to Los Angeles and pose for more of them videos, but I tell him that ain't gonna happen. I tell him my feet are gonna stay retired, and he'll have to get used to that.

I already told you I'm living back in Turkey Roost, Kentucky. Ma she gave me the family farmhouse when she went into a nursing home. That happened last month after Pa took off for Branson, Missouri. He went there to join a country band, and he's busy getting famous. I don't hardly hear from Pa no more, and I don't see much of Ma. Ma she's pushing fifty, and she's got arthritis bad.

Turkey Roost is more depressing than ever 'cause the strip mines are all closed down. Donald Trump said he would keep the mines open, so the whole town voted for him, but I don't see a whole lot of evidence that's ever gonna happen. The union headquarters are all bordered up, and most everyone's on the dole. Of course, that ain't the Donald's fault—the man is a living saint. 'Cept for maybe his pussy grabbing and all them Twitter rants. Anyway, the air's a whole lot cleaner, and that's gotta count for something.

I'm married now. Did you know that? I got wed to Benny Pearman who was in my graduating class at Turkey Roost High School. Benny he got a job at a Sam's Club down in Nashville. He don't work there no more though 'cause he broke his hip moving boxes. So what he does now is play Fantasy Baseball and draw a disability pension. I ain't exactly sure why I married Benny—he just kinda proposed a few months ago, and I didn't see much reason to say no. But I kinda wish I'd held out for a dude named Tommy Lee Weaver. Tommy Lee starred alongside me when I was in our high school production of *Annie*. He played Daddy Warbucks, and he hadda wear a swimming cap so he could look like he was bald. His hair is thick and redder 'an a chestnut, and I saw it peeking out of his swimming cap when we were singin' together on stage. Tommy Lee also wrote a poem that got published in the school newspaper. And he gave me a buncha black-eyed Susans after the final performance of *Annie*. I ain't been in touch with Tommy Lee since he went to Eastern Kentucky University in Richmond. He said he was gonna further his education, so he can be a pharmacist.

After Benny and I got married, I went to work at a Walmart in Bowling Green. My job was to stand at the entrance and greet folks comin' in. I'm real good at that 'cause I got a nice smile and my hair is dyed strawberry blonde. I don't work there no more though 'cause Walmart shut itself down. That happened after the United Auto Workers tried to start up a union there. So what I do now is buy lottery tickets and find reasons to get out of the house. I kinda wish I had never married Benny—he just parks himself in our Barcalounger, sips beer and play made-up baseball. I kinda wish I had gone to Richmond and moved in with Tommy Lee.

Well, you can only buy so many lottery tickets and you can only do so much pining. So I decided that maybe it was time that I started up my own business. Like I told ya, I'm real good at making dresses—I sewed all the costumes for *Annie*. So I set up a shop in this ol' barn that sits behind the house. The Nose, he still sends me royalty checks, and I used them to start things up. I bought a dozen bolts of fabric and a Singer sewing machine and one of them torso dummies to fit the dresses on. After I made me a buncha dresses, I took pictures of 'em with my cell phone. And I put the pictures on a website that read *Frocks by Gertie McDowell, Stage Star and Impromptu Artist*. And I sent the link to that pervert site that the Nose set up for me.

Well, even though I'm kinda famous, I only got one dress order. Patty Bill Willis, who runs an egg farm near Coon Creek, asked me to make an Easter dress for her ten-year-old granddaughter. I ain't never made no Easter Dress, so I went on the internet, checked a few of 'em out, and printed out one of the pictures. Easter dresses have real high waists and they don't have no bust at all, and they got so many ruffles that they're practically Christmas tree shaped. Well, I made a cute little Easter dress, and it fit Patty Bill's granddaughter perfect. Patty Bill said her granddaughter was gonna be the best-dressed girl at the egg hunt.

I charged Patty Bill forty dollars, which I thought was pretty reasonable, but Patty Bill just looked at me like I was trying to pick her pocket. She didn't pay me no money, but she gave me about six-dozen eggs. So every night for a week, I fixed omelets with hominy grits.

*

THERE AIN'T MUCH POINT in being famous if it don't bring you no business. Heck, I checked my website every day for a month, but I didn't get no more dress orders. Benny Pearman said it's probably 'cause I ain't reached my demographic. He said my fans on the internet—the ones that watch me grab worms with my toes—ain't likely to buy anything but DVD pornography. So I put together an email pitch and linked it to my website, and I sent it to all the women's wear distributors I could find on the internet. I didn't get no replies 'cept one from Coldwater Creek. All they wanted to do was send me a catalog.

Well, a coupla months later, I'd pretty much decided to close my business down. That's when an opportunity came knockin' like a sinner at heaven's door. This email popped up in my mailbox from a retailer called Sugar Shack Trends. I ain't never heard of that company, but I think it has foreign roots. It was sent by a gentleman named Jean Valjean who musta been a Frenchman.

Dear Miss McDowell, the letter read. *Your daring hemlines and use of lace have come to our attention. Would you consider joining our distributorship and enhancing the Sugar Shack brand? We are a rapidly growing company with outlets all over America, and we would be honored if you would consider becoming one of our designers. Congratulations on being invited to join the Sugar Shack family.*

Well, I read the email a coupla times, and my heart started to pound like a mallet. Shucks, I ain't never been invited to join no family. The only family I got now is Ma, and she ain't the joining type. She just sits in her room in the nursing home and watches *Frasier* reruns on TV. So I sent an email to Jean Valjean, thanking him for the offer. And I said that as long as it didn't cost me no money, I'd be proud to promote his brand.

It weren't but fifteen minutes before that gentleman emailed me back. He said I had made a wise move that was going to change my life. He said his company only hires the most promising designers, and then he went on to explain to me how things were going to work. He said I would be responsible for making the dresses and taking them to the customers, and his company would be responsible for quality control. He also said my work was so beautiful that I needed to keep a low profile. He said there were plenty of imitators out there that would steal my designs if they could.

There was a contract attached to the email, which was kinda hard to read, so I emailed the contract to the Nose 'cause I value his opinion. The Nose he called me on my cell phone and gave me some advice. He said he had never heard of the company, and I oughta proceed with caution. He suggested I test the waters before dipping in my toes.

Well, I emailed that fella named Jean Valjean and asked if I could have a trial run. He said that would be no problem, and that he admired my business savvy. He instructed me to make a red cocktail dress for a woman in Beaver Creek, and he sent me the woman's measurement and told me to do my best work.

Since I wanted to make a good impression, I ordered this real neat fabric. The fabric was stretch satin and it shimmered like a ruby, and the texture was so smooth and slinky that it electrified my palm. Well, I made a cocktail dress using an example I found on the internet. 'Cept I gave it a plunging neckline and I kept the hemline low, and I put a slit in the side of the dress to give it a sexy look. When I was done, it was all I could do not to bawl like a week-old calf. The dress was so beautiful it looked like an angel oughta wear it.

I mailed the dress to Jean Valjean's post office box for its quality inspection. A few days later, the dress came back looking more beautiful than ever. The company had added some lace to the neck and put in some fancy pleats, and the Sugar Shack label, featuring a picture of a cottage, was sewn into the neckline. A note was pinned to the dress, and it said I did a wonderful job. The note listed the address of the woman who was gonna buy my dress.

Well, I put the dress in a garment bag and I hung it in the back of my Jeep, and I drove an hour to Beaver Creek to make my delivery. Beaver Creek is a gutted farm town that only has one street, so it took me only a minute to find my customer's house.

The woman who answered my knock on the door was kinda dried-up and old, so I ain't sure what she wanted with a brand new cocktail dress. But I gave her the dress in the garment bag and she gave me a weary smile, and she handed me an envelope and told me to count the money.

I counted out five hundred dollars in fifty-dollar bills, and I told the woman I wasn't expectin' to get paid quite so much. She told me she'd seen my site on the internet and admires the work I'd done. She said she don't mind paying top dollar for such beautiful designs.

Before she went back into the house, the woman patted my cheek. She told me to have a wonderful day, and that it was an honor to make my acquaintance. And she assured me it wouldn't be long until I became a famous dress designer.

Well, with all that cash in my wallet, I felt richer 'an Bill Gates. And that woman she sure made my day when she said I was gonna be famous. But it seemed sorta odd that she paid for the dress without even trying it on.

*

WHEN I GOT HOME and checked my email, there was another message from Jean Valjean. He said the customer who bought my dress had told all her friends about me. He said my reputation was spreading, and he had another dress order for me. He said a woman from Rocky Mound—a town in Tennessee—wanted me to make her a black maxi dress with a split. He also said it was the thrill of his life to be representing me, and that he was gonna reduce his commission to only forty percent.

Well, I sent an email to Jean Valjean, telling him what the cocktail dress fetched, and he told me to put two hundred dollars in an envelope and send it to his post office box. He said the rest of the money was mine 'cause I'd done such a wonderful job. He also advised me to keep things hush-hush—at least until he secured a patent for everything I designed.

Shucks, I felt kinda sad that I couldn't go out and celebrate my success. But if you're gonna *stay* successful, you can't be slacking off. So I went online and found a picture of a real cool maxi dress, and I ordered a bolt of duchess satin 'cause I wanted the dress to shine. When the satin arrived, I gasped like a faucet—it practically blinded me. I couldn't believe how light hit the fabric and bounced right offa it.

I followed the basic design of the dress then I made a couple of changes. I cut the back away and I left one shoulder bare then I shortened the hemline a bit so the customer could show off her ankles. I worked all through the night on the dress 'cause I completely lost track of time. By the time I was done, the first light of dawn came leakin' through the window. The way the fabric glowed in the morning light made my knees feel kinda wobbly. It truly looked like the dress had been touched by the hand of God.

Well, I mailed the dress to that Sugar Shack company for its quality inspection, and a few days later the dress came with a note from Jean Valjean. He wrote that the dress was a masterpiece—a garment fit for a queen—and that an angel musta guided my hands when I put the dress together. He also said that inspecting my work was like worshipping at a shrine, so he was gonna cut his commission down to just thirty percent.

*

I KINDA WISH the hand of God would do something 'bout Benny Pearman. 'Cause Benny he started lecturing me about all the time I spent makin' dresses. He said a marriage is gonna suffer if a couple don't spend time together. Well, since Benny has nothing to offer me but beer and Fantasy Baseball, I told him our marriage was already suffering as much as it needed to. I said if I gave up making dresses, it would suffer a whole lot worse. So I bought Benny a super-wide Flat-Screen TV and I got him a case of Budweiser, and I told him to enjoy himself 'cause I had a delivery to make.

I drove two hours to Rocky Mound, another boarded up mining town, and I delivered the dress to a square-jawed woman who mighta been a transvestite. Her arms were kinda muscular and her chest was kinda sunken, so for a moment I was worried that I made the bust too large. But the woman she just smiled at me and called me a lovely child. And she handed me an envelope fulla hundred dollar bills.

The woman she asked me to count the money before she accepted the dress, so I counted the hundred dollar bills and there was ten of them. I felt my knees start to buckle and I felt real light in the head, and if the woman hadn't caught me I'd have toppled off her porch. When I told her she'd paid too much for the dress, she winked and shook her head. She said my reputation precedes me and not to sell myself short.

As I drove back to Kentucky, I was shaking like a drunk; it was all I could do to keep the Jeep from driftin' off the highway. So I parked the Jeep in Opryland, which is just outside of Nashville, and I treated myself to a fancy dinner of pork chops and collard greens. By the time I got back to Turkey Roost, it was ten o'clock at night, but I stopped at the post office anyhow and I stretched 'til I heard my neck crack. After that, I mailed three of them hundred dollar bills to that Sugar Shack company.

*

WELL, I SIGNED that Sugar Shack contract and dress orders kept stacking up, and I spent every waking minute making dresses and delivering them. I didn't deliver the dresses 'til I first sent them to Jean Valjean 'cause he told me he was havin' 'em professionally photographed to show in a catalog. I never saw the catalogue, but he said it looked real great.

Benny he got in my face one day and gave me an ultimatum. He told me I hadda choose—it was either them dresses or him. I told him that weren't no contest at all and to not let the door hit his ass when he left. So Benny moved in with his mother and mailed me some divorce papers, and after I had a good cry I sent a text message to Tommy Lee Weaver. I asked Tommy Lee how he was doin' and I asked if he still wrote poems, and I told him he looked really silly when he was wearin' that bathing cap. Tommy Lee he called me back and said he was doin' fine. He said he was in a relationship now and a baby was on the way, and he said he remembered the fun we had when both of us starred in *Annie*. I wished Tommy Lee the best of luck, and I'm sure I meant it too. You can't begrudge no happiness to a man who played Daddy Warbucks.

Well, I kept on making dresses and I banked almost all of my profits, and it weren't too long before I had thirty thousand dollars in my account. But makin' dresses is lonely work, so I phoned the Nose every night. The Nose he told me not to fret 'cause you just can't hurry love. He said one day my prince will come, and I gotta be patient 'til then. And he promised to send me some peep-toe stilettos to wear on my wedding day.

I thanked the Nose for his kind advice even though it was pretty corny. Just 'cause a fella's a prince don't mean that I'll wanna take up with him. What if he's as bald as a billiard ball or has ears like England's Prince Charles? But maybe he'll be like

Jean Valjean who sounds real suave in his emails. Mr. Valjean sounds like a Latin gentleman with frost around his temples, and I'll bet he's been all over the world and made love to a whole lotta women. So I sent an email to Jean Valjean, and I thanked him for all his support. And I said he oughta give me a knock if he's ever in Turkey Roost. I said maybe we could go to a Cracker Barrel and have us some chicken and dumplings.

Well, Jean Valjean he emailed me back. He said he'd be honored to meet me, but we can't be seen dining together. He said there are fashion spies everywhere and we gotta watch out for them, 'cause one of them moles might follow me home and steal all my designs. But he promised to send me a bracelet with the Sugar Shack logo on it. And he said when he got all my patents secured, we might have us a meal together. He said he's real fond of chicken and dumplings and likes to eat collard greens too.

*

MONTHS WENT BY and I never got no visit from Jean Valjean. But I made and delivered a whole lotta dresses, and the money kept pourin' in. I made dirndl dresses and tunic dresses and baby doll dresses with lace. I made slip-on dresses and granny dresses and even a coupla caftans. And I delivered the dresses all over Kentucky and most of Tennessee. I delivered 'em to quaint little towns that looked like time had forgot 'em. Places with names like Possum Hollow, Goose Valley, and Gopher Hill. Places with shutdown union halls and stores with empty window fronts. But, although the towns looked like they'd seen better days, my clients all welcomed me. A lot of 'em gave me a hug and called me a lovely child. The way they looked at me, you'd have thought all their Christmases had come.

Well, my partnership with that Sugar Shack company ended a little abruptly. But you probably already guessed that this was gonna happen. One day, I was making a corset dress—a dress with tight lace around the middle—when I heard this knockin' on the door of the barn where my workshop was set up. The knockin' was kinda rapid, like a woodpecker was makin' a hole, so I was kinda surprised when I opened the door and saw a gentleman standing there. The gentleman was dressed in a business suit and his hair was brown with white flecks in it, and he looked so dapper and sexy that my heart leaped like a frog.

"Would you like some supper?" I said to him. "I could make you some chicken and dumplings."

The gentleman blushed redder 'an a cherry tomato—he seemed to be kinda embarrassed. But his manners were so elegant that he reminded me of George Clooney. He said "please" when he told me to turn around and place my hands behind my back, and he put the handcuffs on me so careful it felt like he was slipping on bracelets. He even asked me to watch my step when he walked me to his car, and he said that he hoped them cuffs weren't gripping my wrists too tight.

The gentleman drove me to Bowling Green where they got a federal courthouse, and all the way there we chatted like we were a couple of old friends. I asked him if he was married, and he told me he was divorced—he said that being a DEA agent was kind of hard on a marriage. I asked him if he had children and he said he had two girls, and he saw them every weekend and took them to their soccer games. He asked me how come I got involved in dealing powdered meth, and when I said I didn't know nothing 'bout that, he patted me on the shoulder. He told me I shoulda checked the hems before I delivered them dresses.

When he dropped me off at the Warren County Jail, we were as close as two pups in a litter. He shook my hand after removing the cuffs, and he said he hoped things worked out for me. So I asked him to look me up once I was out of jail. I told him I'd never fault him for being a federal agent. I told him I thought I would make him a real devoted wife.

*

WELL, I'M STUCK IN the Federal Prison Camp in Alderson, West Virginia. The trial it didn't go too well, so I'm gonna be here awhile. When I told the judge what happened, he thought I was pulling his leg. He said Jean Valjean is a character in a Broadway musical. He said Sugar Shack ain't no company, it's the name of a popular song. He also told me that court ain't no place to be telling whoppers that big and that if I thought I was getting away with them, I was dumber than broccoli. So he gave me five years for trafficking drugs and sent me to Alderson, and he said he hoped I'd use the time to ponder my crooked ways.

They call this place Camp Cupcake 'cause Martha Stewart once stayed here. And I gotta admit the inmates are nice and the guards are real polite. I'm sharing a two-bunk cell with a woman named Bertha Jean, and Bertha let me join a gang of women that she calls her family. My job is in the sewing shop, where they make clothes for federal inmates, and I kinda like the assignment 'cause it helps me pass the time. I also like strolling the grounds 'cause the place looks like a college campus.

On Christmas, I got a card from that agent that busted me. He said he hoped I was doing well, and we'll have coffee when I get out. He said he thought I was a really nice girl that just got led astray. I also got a lot of letters from the Nose. The Nose said I'm as trusting as a lamb, and he shoulda advised me better. He said he was gonna find a lawyer to help me with an appeal. He also said he cries every day 'cause I'm just like a daughter to him.

Well, I thanked the Nose for all his concern, but I ain't sure I got fooled all that bad. I shoulda known that Sugar Shack ain't no name for a dress company. I shoulda known that Frenchmen eat frog legs and don't like chicken and dumplings. And I shoulda known there's no market for satin in towns named Beaver Creek. Maybe I'm dumber than broccoli but, dern it, I shoulda known.

3. Crossing the Jordan

HI, IT'S ME AGAIN, Gertie McDowell. Guess it's time I got back to you if you ain't grown tired of me yet. Yes, I'm still at the Federal Prison Camp in Alderson, West Virginia—the place they call Camp Cupcake 'cause Martha Stewart once stayed here. I've served five months of my five-year sentence, and they moved me into one of the cottages. They put me in a two-person room along with Bertha Jean. Bertha Jean she's a great big woman who's doing time for mail fraud. She's all the time writing stories, which ain't been published yet, but she says that one day she'll write a whole novel and sell it to Hollywood.

Bertha Jean let me join a pack of women inmates that she calls her family. Bertha Jean she's kinda the father, and a woman named Wanda Sue is the mother. And there's five younger women who quarrel like sisters, but they do what Bertha Jean says. I'm the youngest one of them all, so I guess that makes me the princess.

I'm still working in the sewing shop, making clothes for federal inmates. And Bertha Jean works in the kitchen where she dishes out food during meals. Whenever I get in the serving line, Bertha Jean gives me a wink. And she gives me extra servings of pork chops, mashed potatoes and collard greens.

In the evening, after dinner, we all meet at some picnic tables. We do a whole lotta chatting there, and some of the women cry a bit. Most of my prison family are mothers even though they're really young. They say the worst thing 'bout being in prison is that they can't be with their kids.

We play a whole lotta checker too, and I wanna say something 'bout that. My dad he taught me how to play checkers before he took off for Branson, Missouri. My dad's a really good checker player—he used to play for money—but it got so I could beat him four games outta five.

When I play checkers with my prison family, I also win most of my games. We don't got much money to bet with, so we usually play for tampons. I've won a whole lotta tampons and I used to just give 'em away, but Bertha Jean she told me that I hadda stop doing that. Bertha Jean runs her own private store that sells tampons, cookies and soap. She said nobody will buy her tampons if I'm giving mine away for free. I charge fifty cents for a tampon now, so's not to undercut Bertha Jean. And when no one's looking, I turn over my profits to the prison library fund.

Almost all of the women here are in relationships with one another. You see 'em holding hands on their beds and fixing each other's hair. A coupla women told me they'd like to be my squeeze, but that sorta stuff don't set too well with a girl from Turkey Roost. 'Sides, I'm saving myself for Agent Jackson, the cop that busted me. He sent me a really nice card on Christmas, and I sent him a box of ginger snaps. I mailed it to the US Drug Enforcement Administration in Louisville 'cause I don't got his home address. And I told him to come look me up once I get outta prison.

Sometimes, at night when everyone's sleeping, I have a bit of a cry. That's 'cause I get kinda lonesome in spite of my new family. I do get letters from Ma, but she ain't come to visit me yet. Dad he ain't come to visit me neither—he says he's on a mission. He says he's gonna find Jean Valjean and beat the shit out of him. So when I get to feeling sorry for myself, I think about Agent Jackson. I think about what a gentleman he was when he arrested me, and

I think about how sad he is 'cause his ex-wife cut him loose. Guess she couldn't handle the fact that he's got such a dangerous job.

When I think about Agent Jackson, I feel kinda weak in my water. Agent Jackson he told me that he'd like to have coffee with me. And who knows what coffee will lead to with a gentleman that fine? I might end up giving him a loving home and maybe a coupla children. Shucks, I'm sure I could make him a real devoted wife.

*

ONE AFTERNOON, when I was playing checkers, the warden walked up to our picnic table. His name is Warden Jordan, and he's a great big sociable fella. He looks sorta like John Candy and he's always cracking jokes, and it's funny when he looks at you 'cause he's got a lazy eye. Bertha Jean says we're lucky to have a superintendent like Warden Jordan. She said serving time is a bitch if you got a prick for a warden. I guess Bertha Jean oughta know 'cause she's been in three different prisons.

Well, Warden Jordan he stood by the table and watched me crown a king. And then he rolled back on his heels and gave me a real strange look. But it's always strange when he looks at you on account of his lazy eye. "Sweets," he said in a voice fulla fun, "is what they're telling me true?"

"I ain't sure what they're telling you, sir," I said to him real polite. "If I don't know what they're telling you, I dunno if the telling is true."

Warden Jordan he smiled at me, then he patted me on the wrist. "What they're telling me, Miss McDowell, is that you've been putting on airs. They say you're calling yourself the checker champion of all of Alderson prison."

Well, if I was gonna call myself something, it wouldn't be a checker champion. 'Cause winning a buncha tampons ain't much to boast about. So I said to Warden Jordan, "Sir, I ain't never put on no airs. Not even when I was a video star and a famous dress designer."

Warden Jordan he shuffled his feet like maybe his bunions hurt. All the time, he kept staring at me with his creepy lazy eye. He said, "Sweets, it doesn't *matter* if you call yourself a champion or not. Other women are calling you that, which only makes matters worse."

Well, I said to Warden Jordon, "Sir, I'm serving five years for drug sales. I don't see how playing checkers is gonna make matters worse."

"It's not about playing checkers," the warden said with a laugh. "It's about people treating you like a queen when you haven't earned your crown."

"Whatcha mean by that?" I said as I capped another king.

"What I mean by *that*," the warden said, "is that I'm putting a bug in your ear. Unless you can beat me four games out of seven, your glory days are over."

"You wanna play checkers with *me*?" I said 'cause I couldn't believe what I heard. For a moment, I thought he was telling me he was gonna give me lice.

But the warden he said to come to his office the following afternoon. He said it was high time I learned a little humility. And he told me that he's the best damn checker player in all of Monroe County.

After the warden waddled away, Bertha Jean said to be careful. She said Warden Jordan is a pretty good guy, but I oughta keep my distance. She said if I spend too much time with him, some of the women might think I'm a snitch.

Wanda Sue, she just flared her nostrils like maybe I farted in church. Even though she's doing time for robbin' a bank, Wanda Sue's got a streak of religion. "Don't be crossing the Jordan"—that's what she said to me. It weren't 'til several weeks later that I figured out what that meant.

*

WELL, THE FOLLOWING AFTERNOON, I reported to Warden Jordan's office. He has a mighty nice office over in the administration building. It's got a fancy mahogany desk and a leather executive chair, and there was pictures all over the walls of fashion models showing off dresses. There was pictures of models in tunic dresses and baby doll dresses and caftans. There was pictures of models wearing fit-and-flare dresses and even some mini sheaths. I have to admit it was kinda weird to see all them fashion photos, but I gotta say that when it comes to dresses the warden has real good taste.

Warden Jordan said to have a seat on the opposite side of his desk. He had already set up the checkerboard, and he told me I could have the first move. He said that to make it interesting, we could have us a little wager. If I beat him four games out of seven, he'd give me a new pair of shower shoes. And if he took the series offa me, I would have to make his wife a dress. The warden said he was real impressed that I was a dress designer. And he said he was sorry I weren't more careful in screening out my clients.

Well, I ain't too sure how smart it was to bet with Warden Jordan. But we shook hands on the bet and we played the first game, and I beat him in just twenty-one moves. Warden Jordan said I took an unfair advantage 'cause I waited too long to move. So he put an egg timer on the desk and set it for ninety seconds. He said if I took longer than that to move, I would have to forfeit the game. Well, I kept my moves to under a minute, and I won the next game even faster. And Warden Jordan he looked at me like I was some kinda haunt.

"Miss McDowell" he muttered, "have I underestimated you?"

Well, I didn't want to rub it in—I could see his pride was hurt. Shucks, I felt like I did the day Ma caught me swipin' her coconut-scented shampoo. "Don't fault yourself for doubting me," I said to

Warden Jordan. "If you're the best checker player in all Monroe County, that's gotta be easy to do."

Warden Jordan he opened his desk drawer and pulled out a handkerchief. And he cleaned off all of his checker pieces as though they were covered with ants. "Miss McDowell," he said with a sneer, "you have two more games to win. I don't want none of your sympathy unless you win another two games."

Well, I pretended to be befuddled and I lost the next four games, and that was kinda hard to do 'cause the warden made some really dumb moves. But I didn't throw them games 'cause I was scared of Warden Jordan—he's a really sociable fella and he's got great taste in fashion. I blew them games 'cause it didn't make sense to be playing for shower shoes. Not when I could be making a dress for Warden Jordan's wife.

*

AFTER PUTTING AWAY the checker set and grinning like a raccoon, Warden Jordan told me to make his wife a fancy carnival dress. He said him and his wife was going to Mardi Gras in New Orleans, and his wife wanted a dress so colorful she could march in the parade. He said to make her a purple dress with a tangerine-colored bodice, and to also make her a carnival hat that was fulla ostrich feathers. The warden hadn't mentioned no hat when we made ourselves our bet, but I told him he'd won our bet so well that I'd throw in the hat for free.

The warden wrote down some measurements, and I gaped like a carp outta water. His wife was as big as a breeding sow and she didn't have much of a bust, and I was gonna need a whole lotta fabric to whip up a dress that big. I said to the warden it might cost him less if she wore a tent instead.

Well, the warden he ordered some cotton fabric and it took 'bout a week to arrive, and when it arrived I began work on the dress in the prison sewing shop. I made the dress real careful 'cause there weren't no fabric to waste, and I put some pleats and ruffles in it to give it a carnival look. The time it passed real pleasant while I was working on the dress—'cept that the women in the shop kept interrupting me to ask me what I was doing. Well, I couldn't tell 'em I was making a dress for the warden's wife to wear. Shucks, even in Camp Cupcake, you don't wanna look like no snitch. So I told 'em I was crossing the Jordan—it was all I could think of to say.

*

IT TOOK ME A WEEK to finish the dress 'cause I hadda use a whole lotta stitches, and word about what I was doing got back to my prison family. Bertha Jean said that something weren't right, and she told me I better be careful. She said Warden Jordan musta found a way to take advantage of me. Wanda Sue she just clucked her tongue and called me a foolish child. She said whatever I was up to, I was gonna reap what I sowed. But Warden Jordan he beamed like a bride when I finally gave him the dress. He said I could have them shower shoes even though I lost the bet.

When the ostrich feathers arrived in the mail, I went to work on the hat. And them women in the sewing shop looked at me like I was crazy. They wanted to know why I was making a hat that only a stripper would wanna wear. "I'm crossing the Jordan," I told 'em, and I didn't say nothing more.

After I gave Warden Jordan the hat, he planted a smooch on my knuckles. And he said he was gonna write the Federal Parole Commission and tell 'em I was a model inmate. He said he was gonna ask the Parole Commission to grant me an early release.

When I told Bertha Jean about this, she frowned like a hanging judge. She said federal parole was eliminated more 'an forty years ago. She also said Warden Jordan was running a con on me. Either that or he hadda be six fries short of a Happy Meal.

Well, I didn't have no reason to be doubtin' Bertha Jean. Bertha Jean's been good to me and she made me part of her family and, whenever I go through the serving line, she gives me extra helpings. Even so, I wrote Agent Jackson and told him what the warden promised. I said it might not be too long 'til I could have coffee with him.

*

AFTER I GAVE WARDEN JORDAN the hat, he stopped showing up at the prison. At first, I thought that he had gone to New Orleans, so his wife could be in that parade. But a coupla days later, the women were told to report to the prison chapel. That's where we was introduced to this fella who was gonna be our new warden. His name was Claus Von Becker and he looked as mean as a miser, and he made us all stand at attention while he gave us a really stern speech. He told us the prison had gotten too lax and he was gonna tighten things up and, when he was done, it wouldn't be known as Camp Cupcake anymore. There would be no more public displays of affection or running private stores, and no one was gonna be allowed to play checkers for tampons no more. When Mr. Becker was done with his speech, we walked out of the chapel like zombies. All of us was wondering what happened to Warden Jordan. Bertha Jean she speculated that Warden Jordan had found greener pastures. She said running a prison was no kinda job for a fun-lovin' fella like him.

A coupla weeks later, I found out what happened to Warden Jordan. I was watching television in the cottage—me and my family—when an exposé on Warden Jordan popped up on the six o'clock local news. He was in a bar called Swinging Moses', which was somewhere in downtown Charleston, and he was sashaying around on a stage and singin' "I Gotta Be Me." He was wearing the hat I made for his wife, the one with ostrich feathers, and he also had on the carnival dress his wife was supposed to wear. It looked like Warden Jordan had found him the Promised Land, but I wished I had hemmed the dress some more 'cause it was draggin' at his feet.

*

WELL, IT DON'T LOOK LIKE I'm gonna be getting no early release from prison. Maybe that's 'cause I reaped what I sowed—that's what Wanda Sue warned me would happen. Shucks, I ain't even popular with the other women no more. Don't none of 'em wanna play checkers with me—not even if I spot them two pieces. But Bertha Jean she told me I was still part of her family. She said it really weren't my fault that we now have a prick for a warden. And Wanda Sue said I weren't to blame for being as dumb as an oyster. She said the good Lord would protect me 'cause I know not what I do.

When I wrote Agent Jackson and told him what happened, he sent me a really nice letter. He told me I'm a good-hearted girl who keeps getting led astray. He said to hold my head up and to keep my good intentions. He said when I get outta prison, he'll be proud to have coffee with me.

4. The Pig in the Pen

HI, IT'S GERTIE MCDOWELL again, and I hope we're friends by now. And I hope my stories ain't shocking you 'cause that means I'll be shocking you more. Ma always says I tell folks too much, and I guess that's justified. But there ain't no percentage in being well-bred if that means I can't tell my stories.

I'm still at Alderson Prison, and I've done eight months of my sentence. I ain't in the sewing shop no more, Warden Becker took me out of there. He said I had no business sewing a dress for a gender bender. He also took away the good time I'd earned, which came to seventeen days. He said good time means you obey the rules and keep your nose to the grindstone—it don't mean you do personal projects, so's to have yourself a good time. Well, at least I got a pair of shower shoes out of it, and I wear them all the time. That's 'cause I caught athlete's foot in the showers, so I need to air out my feet.

I'm assigned to the prison infirmary now, and I've been there for almost two months. They got me emptying bedpans, mopping the floor and wheeling in meals from the kitchen. I also read to the hospital patients, and that helps pass the time. Their favorite book is this racy novel called *Fifty Shades of Grey*. It's about a woman who takes up with a guy who turns her into a sex slave. I don't much approve of the book but the women really like it, so I think about something else while I'm reading them that smut.

A couple of 'em also like this book called *Call Me Pomeroy*. It's an autobiography wrote by this fella who thinks he's God's gift to women. The guy's a rap musician and he sings about ants in his pants, and he's got the biggest potty mouth that I have ever heard. I hope I never meet this guy 'cause he'd probably call me a spinner, but I doubt that a fella that famous would turn up in Turkey Roost. If that ever happens, I'll ask him to keep a civil tongue in his head.

I ain't heard from Agent Jackson since he wrote me two months back. I suspect that's 'cause he's really busy putting them bad guys in jail. Anyhow, he said he'll have coffee with me when I get outta prison, and a promise from Agent Jackson is a promise you can take to the bank. I hope we can meet at that Starbucks in Nashville that's close to Opryland—it's a really ritzy place that serves bagels and raspberry scones.

The Nose he still writes me a coupla times a month. He says that I got railroaded and the judge oughta be ashamed, and that he's started up a defense fund so that I can appeal my case. He says he don't have much money now 'cause my website is losing fans, and he wishes I could get furloughed so he could make new videos of my feet. He also said Warden Jordan has got him a video on YouTube. It was shot in this bar called The Rainbow, which is somewhere in San Francisco, and it shows him mincing around in that dress and singing "Let's Get It On." The Nose says he don't mind exhibitionists, but he don't like Warden Jordan. He says he's got no use for men who leads young girls astray.

*

NOW I GOTTA TELL YOU 'bout this guy who works in the infirmary. His name is Billy Bacon and he's a spindly little fella with a goatee, and he's always spittin' tobacco juice into a coffee cup. Billy he works as an orderly, which kinda makes him my boss, and he's really conscientious when he ain't spittin' tobacco juice. He's all the time washing patients and taking their vital signs and filling out these charts that hang on the foot of their beds. He even noticed my athlete's foot, and he gave me some fungal cream for it. He said if I apply it three times a day, it will clear up the flaking real quick.

Sometimes, when things are slow, I chat with Billy Bacon. He says he thinks he knows me from somewhere 'cause my face is real familiar. Well, I didn't mention the Nose's website though that's probably where he saw me. I told him I once was a theater star, and maybe he saw me on stage.

Billy told me he don't go to the theater 'cause the theater is too pretentious. He says he watches *WrestleMania* instead and listens to bluegrass music. He says he's got him a bluegrass band that plays in nursing homes, and he thinks the band could go real far if it had a lead vocalist. He's listened to me singing, while I empty out the bedpans, and he says the Lord has blessed me with a voice that's clearer than glass. He said that, when I get out of prison, I oughta join his band. He said we just might end up performing at the Grand Old Opry.

I told Billy Bacon that sounded real nice, and that I'm fonda bluegrass songs. I'm especially fonda "Rocky Top" and "Keep on the Sunny Side of Life." I don't like "Pig in a Pen" too much, and I told Billy Bacon that. That's a song about a travelin' dude who's real proud of his pig, and he wants to marry a pretty little girl who will feed it while he's gone. I told Billy Bacon that that kinda song can get a girl riled up. I told him I ain't never gonna stay home and feed nobody's pig.

*

NOW THAT I'VE SERVED eight months of my sentence, I'm gettin' accustomed to things. I don't like gettin' up at 6:00 a.m. in the morning to make my bed for inspection, but I like the time I get to spend with my prison family. We still meet at them picnic tables after work, and we still play a whole lotta checkers. And Bertha Jean she always asks me how my day has been.

Wanda Sue ain't with us no more 'cause she finished serving her sentence. She's living in Indianapolis now, where she's on supervised release. We get a whole lotta postcards from her 'cause she misses us real bad. She says she's thinking of committing an infraction, so she can come back to prison and see us.

I told Bertha Jean that when I finish my time I'm gonna be a bluegrass singer. I told her how Billy Bacon invited me to join his band. I don't think Agent Jackson would object if I have a music career. Agent Jackson's he's a gentleman, he knows how to treat a girl, and I'm sure that he would encourage me to use my God-given gift. I'm sure he wouldn't make me stay home and feed some stupid pig.

Bertha Jean said that sounded real fine, and she's gonna be rootin' for me. And she said she wouldn't mind personally if I sang "Pig in a Pen." Bertha Jean grew up in South Texas, where she lived on a cattle ranch, and she told me her dad bought a pig one day and penned it next to the barn. Bertha Jean said that it was her job to make sure the pig got slopped. She said she didn't mind feedin' it though 'cause the pig had a whole lotta class.

*

BILLY SAYS HE DON'T LIKE the theater much, but he keeps talkin' about *West Side Story*. He said he took a few of its songs and gave them a bluegrass twang. He says any song can be converted to bluegrass, and that makes it sound a lot better. Well, I told Billy Bacon not to twang no Broadway song that's sung by Jean Valjean. 'Cause Jean Valjean he don't deserve to have his songs improved.

We was havin' this chat in the infirmary break room 'cause things was kinda slow, and Billy was spittin' tobacco juice into this big ol' Styrofoam cup. Since Billy was in a listenin' mood, I sat down on a chair beside him. And I told him the story about how Jean Valjean made me look dumber 'an broccoli. When I was done, Billy lifted his cup and hocked a brown loogie into it.

"Babes," he said, he calls everyone babes even women who are thirty years old. "Babes," he said, "I think you and I need to come to an understanding."

"Whatcha mean by that?" I said 'cause I don't much like that word. Benny Pearman used that word a lot before we got divorced. He said, "Gertie, when folks are married, they oughta to come to an understanding." That meant that he just wanted me washing his socks and fixing him biscuits and gravy. Benny Pearman he never wanted to eat nothing but biscuits and sausage gravy. Shucks, waiting on Benny Pearman was worse than slopping a pig.

"I don't need to come to no understanding," I said to Billy Bacon. "What I need is some more of that foot cream 'cause my toes are itchin' real bad."

Billy he blinked like a frog on a log—he weren't in no hurry to speak. He just sucked a tooth and looked at me like I was his little sister.

"Babes," he said to me finally, "we still need to have a talk. If you really know what's best for you, you wouldn't be in prison."

Well, Billy Bacon he had a point, so I poured me a cup of coffee. And I saucered and blowed my coffee while we had ourselves a talk.

Billy said that I'm in prison 'cause justice took a nap. He said gullibility ain't no crime, and the world needs to hear my story. He said he'll make a video of me if I don't mind being filmed, and he'll put it on the internet for the entire world to see.

Well, experience has taught me it ain't always flattering to pose for videos, so I told Billy Bacon a girl needs time to prepare for something like that. I told him to wait 'til I got my hair done in the prison beauty salon. Shucks, there ain't no point in showing the world that I got dark brown roots.

*

I TOLD BERTHA JEAN how Billy Bacon was gonna tell my story on a video. I don't do nothing anymore without checking with Bertha Jean. Bertha Jean said it sounded like a pretty good idea. She said the world oughta know what Jean Valjean done to me. She also agreed that Billy don't need to be fixin' up Jean Valjean's songs. She said a fella like Jean Valjean don't deserve no songs at all.

When I told Bertha Jean that my hair needed fixin', she said not to worry 'bout that. And she arranged it so I could get my hair done in the prison's beauty salon. She hadda give twenty tampons away to a woman who works in the salon, but Bertha Jean said she was happy to help with such an important cause. So I got my hair put in a bob cut and I got it dyed platinum blonde, and the woman inmate who fixed my hair said I looked just like Marilyn Monroe.

I stuffed some sponges into my bra to make sure I looked really sexy, and I told Billy Bacon to get my good side when he was filming me. Well, Billy he followed me around like a weasel tailing a rat. Shucks, every time I turned around he was pointing his cell phone at me. He filmed me emptying bedpans and moppin' up the floor. He filmed me pushing the meal cart and cleaning out toilet bowls. He even filmed me playing checkers with my prison family. Billy said that when I played checkers, I oughta lose more games. He didn't want it to look like I was havin' too good a time.

After a week, Billy Bacon told me he finished making the video. He said he even put in background music to give it a dramatic mood. He said he didn't use "Pig in a Pen" 'cause he knows I don't like that song. He put in "Folsom Prison Blues," which was written by Johnny Cash.

*

IT WEREN'T BUT THREE DAYS LATER that I got a letter from the Nose. It was fulla that fancy language of his, so I weren't quite sure what it meant. But it weren't too hard to figger out that the Nose was real upset. *My daughter, my heart, my muse,* he wrote, *I pen this with tears in my eyes. Oh treachery, thy name is woman. Oh chicanery, thy name is Eve. How could you have betrayed me so, my golden-haired, twinkle-toed child? Et tu, Brute? is hardly enough to convey my broken heart.*

Well, just 'cause the Nose is a pervert don't mean he oughta suffer, so I used my nightly phone call to call him up collect. The Nose he said he spotted me on a website called *Prison Babes,* and the site is fulla videos titled "Miss Twinkle Toes Redux." He said them videos don't show nothing but my feet, and my toes they shoulda been airbrushed 'cause they look all red and chapped. He also said them videos got no artistic merit. The light is too bright, the scope too bland, and thcm shower shoes are trite. He said it looks like I'd been filmed by some ham-handed amateur.

Well, I guess I got my hair done for nothing, and that kinda riled me up. Shucks, Bertha Jean coulda sold them tampons steada giving them away. So I told the Nose that Billie Bacon done sold me a pig in a poke, and I told him my feet were still retired though I gotta wear shower shoes.

The Nose, he calmed down a tad when I gave him this information, but he said he was gonna take action and heads were gonna roll. He said he was gonna sue the prison for copyright infringement.

*

AFTER I TALKED with the Nose, things started happening fast. Warden Becker he called me into his office and told me the jig was up. He said he found out what was going on because the prison taps our phone calls, and he said I wasn't in prison to become no movie star. The Warden assigned me to the kitchen, scrubbing pots and pans, and he said it would serve me right if I got dishpan hands.

Billy Bacon he musta got fired 'cause I never saw him no more. That saved me the chore of explaining to him that I weren't going to sing in his band. That don't mean that I don't wanna star at the Grand Old Opry, but I ain't gonna be part of no bluegrass band if I gotta whore out my feet. There's a streak of lady in me, I guess. Ain't much I can do about that.

A month later, the Nose won his civil suit for copyright infringement. He wrote and told me the case was settled for half a million dollars. I suppose that's 'cause the prison don't want more publicity. It probably got enough of that when Martha Stewart was here.

Well, the Nose used some of that money to hire me an appeals attorney, and a few weeks later, a judgment came down from the Sixth Circuit Court of Appeals. The Court it reversed the decision by that judge in Warren County. It said I lacked the specific intent to be charged with trafficking drugs. I ain't exactly sure what that meant, but I phoned the Nose right away. I said I was beholdin' to him for buying me so much justice, and I told him my feet were still retired and to not get no ideas.

The moment I hung the phone up, I got processed for release. I was given a calico dress to wear and a bus ticket to Turkey Roost and a check for two hundred dollars to take care of my immediate needs. And Warden Becker he shook my hand and wished me the best of luck, and I thanked Warden Becker for helping me see the error of my ways. I also asked him if he would allow me to hang around one more day. I'm sure Bertha Jean woulda thrown me a party with Kool-Aid and commissary cookies. Warden Becker said he wouldn't mind if Bertha Jean threw me a party, but it wouldn't be legal for him to keep me in prison an extra day. He said people gotta respect the law if they wanna turn over a new leaf.

*

I'M LIVING BACK in Turkey Roost now, and things are normal again. I'm staying in the farmhouse Ma gave me, and I'm working part-time at McDonald's. I decided I ain't makin' dresses no more 'cause I don't see no future in that. But I sent a letter to Agent Jackson, telling him I was outta prison. I also told him I might be available to have some coffee with him. I ain't heard from Agent Jackson yet, and it's been a coupla weeks, but that's probably because he's chasin' down all them drug dealers crossin' the border.

There ain't a whole lot else happening here, and I'm starting to get restless again. Shucks, most of the time I just sit on the porch and watch the leaves change color. I miss my prison family and that crazy Warden Jordan, and I especially miss how Bertha Jean took such good care of me. I gotta tell you one more thing, and I hope you don't repeat it. Dern it, there's even times when I miss Billy Bacon.

5. Black-Eyed Peas

HI, IT'S GERTIE MCDOWELL again, and I ain't run outta stuff to tell ya. And I hope you like me enough by now that you'll cut me a little slack. 'Cause my stories are gonna get darker, and I don't wantcha to put the book down.

What I'm gonna tell you now is how I got into the Witness Protection Program. I don't know why they call it a protection program 'cause it don't protect you from much. It don't protect you from feeling lonely or catching a winter cold, and it don't protect you from belching too loud or even from slurping your coffee. It does protect you from keeping your roots and having yourself a home, but the home I had in Turkey Roost didn't amount to nothin'. So I guess it don't really hurt me none to be protected from that.

My new story it starts in Turkey Roost when I weren't expecting nothin' to happen. A month had passed since I was released from the Federal Prison Camp, and I was sitting on the porch of that farmhouse Ma gave me and watching the leaves dry up. I hadn't heard from Agent Jackson though I wrote him a coupla letters, and I even printed my phone number on the back of the envelopes. But at least Bertha Jean been writing me—she sends me a letter a week. She said she's real happy I'm outta prison but she misses me a whole lot, and she hopes we can get together when she's done serving time. Bertha Jean's serving time for mail fraud, and she's a repeat offender, so it's probably gonna be a while 'til she gets outta prison. I been answering all her letters though 'cause she's just like a mother to me. I said I missed our checker games and sharing a room with her, and that I was grateful she gave away all them tampons so I could get my hair done.

Well, I was sitting alone on the porch and I was having a glass of iced tea, and I was feelin' philosophical 'cause autumn wakes up your mind. I weren't thinking about the meaning of life 'cause I ain't sure it's got too much meaning, but I was trying to figger something out that's been bothering me a long time. What I was wondering about was who Cain married when God banished him to the Land of Nod. 'Cause God had only made Adam and Eve when Cain and Able was born, and Cain he killed Able so there weren't hardly no humans left. But Cain he went to the Land of Nod and he had him a son named Enoch, and the Bible don't say a single word about how something like that could happen.

Well, I called the Nose on my cell phone—I call him 'bout once a week—and I asked him how come Cain had a son if there weren't no young females around. The Nose he said he had no idea unless Cain chose to marry an ape. He also told me I had no reason to be worrying my head about that. The Nose he said what I ought to be doing is letting him film my feet, and he invited me to come to Los Angeles and stand in a tub fulla Jell-O.

We was havin' this conversation when I heard the crunchin' of tires, then I saw this black sedan come rolling up my driveway. Normally, I don't think twice about cars when I see them in my driveway 'cause usually it's just city folk who are lost and wanting directions. But this time, I took more notice 'cause the car kinda spoke to me. I could sense that something unusual was coming in my direction.

*

WELL, THE CAR DOOR it slammed like a thunderclap after this dude got out, and the fella he walked towards me like he had some business to discuss. The fella was dark-skinned and kinda short and he looked about forty years old, and he had this heavy mustache that was waxed at both of its ends. I guess the dude was a Mexican, which meant he was probably a rapist. There's hundreds of rapists crossing the border according to Donald Trump, dudes who don't wanna do nothing but rape everything in their path.

Well, the fella he walked right up to my porch and looked at me like he knowed me from somewhere. And when he didn't rip my dress off, I gave him a bit of a smile. Shucks, just 'cause a fella's got Mexican genes don't mean that he'll act upon 'em—not if he goes to church every Sunday and don't get too drunk on tequila.

The fella he gave me a little bow and he smiled at me real polite, and he took off this Stetson hat he was wearing and clutched it against his chest. "Gertrude McDowell?" the fella said, and his voice sounded fulla flowers. He looked like maybe he oughta have starred in *Brokeback Mountain*.

"Wouldja like a glass of iced tea?" I said 'cause I hoped he might become my friend. Shucks, a woman's life ain't really complete unless she's got a gay friend.

"That would be lovely, chica," he said. "How kind you are to offer. Yes, I would love a glass of iced tea if it would not put you to too much trouble."

Well, I decided it weren't no trouble at all to fetch him a glass of iced tea. Shucks, that kinda trouble don't even compare with the trouble of getting raped. So I invited the dude to sit on the porch and I fetched him a glass of iced tea, then I sat on the chair beside him and we had us a little chat.

The dude told me his name was Sancho Panza and he worked as a private detective, and he knew about Jean Valjean and how he'd taken advantage of me. He wanted to know if I needed his help to bring Jean Valjean to justice. He said it was his mission in life to hold criminals to account 'cause local cops are burros too dumb to do their job.

Well, I felt my pulse leap like a grasshopper as this fella kept talking to me. It's exciting to meet a private detective, especially in Turkey Roost. But I told the dude I hadn't given no thought to bringing Jean Valjean to justice. I told him a bigger matter was weighing on my mind, and I asked him to help me figger it out 'cause he looked like he might be Catholic. I asked him if he knew who Cain married when he went to the Land of Nod.

The dude said, "Chica, you think such deep thoughts" and he swirled the iced tea in his glass. "I do not see how anyone could take such advantage of you."

Well, the fella he stared at his glass of iced tea as though examining a crystal ball. It seemed that he was doin' a whole lot of thinkin', so's to come up with an intelligent answer. But after a minute, he raised his head and looked me right in the eye.

"What can it possibly *matter*?" he said. He sounded a tad upset, so I decided it might be appropriate if I let the matter drop.

Well, we chatted for half an hour, and he told me about Jean Valjean. He said Jean Valjean is a lowlife and he oughta be in jail, and he needed some clues to find him 'cause Jean Valjean covers his tracks. He said Jean Valjean has a history of bamboozling folks like me, and anyone who would do such things don't deserve to walk free on the earth.

When the dude was done talking, he took my hand and gave it a little squeeze. "Gertrude," he said. "I do not like that name. May I call you something else?"

Well, I never been crazy 'bout my name either, so that seemed like a good idea. "Whatcha wanna call me?" I said.

The dude he smiled like a coon shucking corn and he swirled the iced tea in his glass, and the cubes they rattled so loud they sounded like dice in a cup. "If you don't mind," the fella said, "I would like to call you Cosette."

*

WELL, IT LOOKED LIKE Sancho Panza and I was gonna be real good friends. 'Cause he popped around every afternoon and sat on my porch with me, and sometimes he brought a bag of bagels that he said he picked up at Kroger. And on them days when he didn't bring no bagels, I fixed us some soft-shelled tacos, and I served 'em with jalapenos 'cause Mexicans like their food spicy.

I really liked talking with Sancho Panza 'cause he could keep a conversation going. Shucks, men who ain't gay are usually done talkin' after 'bout fifty words. But Sancho Panza could talk for hours on just about any subject. I even asked him the meaning of life just to see what he would say.

Sancho Panza he scratched his head. "Ah, little Cosette," he said as he took him a bite of a bagel. "Is that not like asking me the meaning of a turnip?" But he thought a while longer and finished eatin' his bagel then a gleam came into his eye. "Perhaps it is just one thing for each of us," he said, and his voice sounded sorta strange. "Perhaps we must climb every mountain, my dear, until we have found that one thing."

Well, I think Jack Palance said that in a movie called *City Slickers*. Or maybe I don't got my movies straight, and that came from *The Sound of Music*. But I guess it don't really matter where Sancho Panza picked that up. He clearly had some movie culture, and I felt really happy 'bout that.

I also felt happy that Sancho Panza was a really thorough fella. 'Cause he kept askin' me questions 'bout what I knew of the whereabouts of Jean Valjean. He asked if I had Jean Valjean's address or a phone number that might be traced. He asked if I knew any people who might tell me where he could be found. I couldn't answer none of them questions, but I felt good Sancho Panza was so thorough. A girl likes to feel safe from unscrupulous fellas who might try to lead her astray. Shucks, I don't guess no bad guy would stand a chance with Sancho Panza on his trail.

After a week, I wrote Agent Jackson and told him I had a new friend. A friend who was fulla culture and liked to discuss deep things. A friend who looked kinda like Al Pacino, that Mexican in the Godfather movies. I also told Agent Jackson that he needn't be jealous or nothin'. I told him that Sancho Panza was gay, and we didn't do nothin' but philosophize. I told Agent Jackson that, when he had time, I'd still like to have coffee with him.

*

WELL, A COUPLA WEEKS LATER, Sancho Panza and I was watchin' the Turner channel. The channel was showin' *The Godfather I*, and that's one of my favorite movies. I was fixin' fried chicken and black-eyed peas 'cause it was just about suppertime, and my fingers were kinda numb from shelling them black-eyed peas.

Well, I said to Sancho Panza that I hoped he liked black-eyed peas. And I said they oughta call 'em goat peas 'cause that's their actual name. I said the name those peas got now makes it sound like they're spoilin' to fight. And that don't make sense since they're easy to swallow and don't require no soakin'.

Sancho Panza was sitting at the kitchen table, nursing a glass of tequila. I'd bought him a bottle of tequila at Kroger 'cause that's all Mexicans drink. Well, he took him a swig of tequila and he gave me a little wink, then his face it grew all-thoughtful like I'd told him the meaning of life. "Ah, Cosette," he said finally. "Such a funny *mind* you have. I must admit that I never know what you are going to say next."

Well, I never know what I'm gonna say neither, so I guess that makes us even. So I finished shelling them black-eyed peas then I threw 'em in a pan, and I tossed in some bay leaves and bacon rinds so's to give 'em a little flavor. There ain't nothin' like a handful of bacon rinds to liven up black-eyed peas.

Like I said, we was watchin' *The Godfather I* 'cause that's one of my favorite movies. We was watching that part where that Godfather fella managed to get himself shot. And I said to Sancho Panza that the fella was kinda like Jesus. 'Cause them bad guys persecuted him when he wouldn't join no drug cartel.

I weren't lookin' to spark no heated discussion, but that set Sancho Panza off. He took a big gulp of tequila then he slammed his fist on the table, and he said if it weren't for the Church interferin' *nobody* woulda hadda got shot. He said the Godfather woulda sold lotsa drugs if the government hadn't forbid it, and that's 'cause the politicians get ordered around by the Church. He said some laws don't oughta be laws, and the Church oughta burn for that.

"Aye, chica," he said, and his eyes got damp. "Please do not get me wrong. I still go to church every Sunday, I still give money to the poor, and every Easter I still light a candle to the Virgin of Guadeloupe. But the Church has no *right* to interfere with how a man makes his living."

Well, them peas were startin' to bubble and them bacon rinds looked soft and the chicken was hissin' like rattlesnakes, so I took the pans off the stove. And since Sancho Panza seemed kinda tormented, I changed the conversation. I asked him again who Cain married when he went to the Land of Nod. Shucks, a fella as religious as Sancho Panza oughta have an opinion on that.

Sancho Panza he buried his face in his hands, and he said to stop asking that question. He said that he didn't need no more riddles, and I oughtn't be thinkin' about that. He told me I was a wonderful cook, and he thanked me for fixing dinner. And he asked me to dish him up an extra helping of black-eyed peas.

*

WELL, SANCHO PANZA never spoke again 'bout who Cain went and married. But the next day he opened up a pocket Bible and quoted from the Book of Matthew. "'Come with me,'" he recited, "'and I will make thee fishers of men.'" At that time, we was fishing for bluegills over at Miller's Pond 'cause Sancho Panza had mentioned that he was really fonda fishing. I had bought us some cartons of bee moth grubs 'cause winter was comin' on early, and when the water's cold them bluegills won't bite on nothin' else.

We was sittin' under a maple tree and we had caught us a buncha bluegills, and we was holdin' 'em in a minnow trap so the turtles wouldn't gobble 'em up. And I said to Sancho Panza, I ain't never fished for no men, but when I was a girl I waded the criks and hogged me some buffalo catfish. "They ain't as tasty as bluegill," I said, "and ya gotta bleed 'em quick, but if you cook 'em in butter and garlic, they make a real sweet fry."

Sancho Panza he laughed and said, "Ah, Cosette, you never fail to surprise me." And he told me this plan he thought up to capture Jean Valjean. He asked me to email Jean Valjean and tell him I still wanted to be partners. And also to tell him that weren't gonna happen 'til I met with him face-to-face. "Pick a restaurant or bar," Sancho Panza said, "and ask him to meet you there. The moment he walks in to talk with you, I will place him under arrest."

Well, I said to Sancho Panza that that sounded really sneaky, and Sancho Panza he opened his Bible and read more from the Book of Mathew. He read where Jesus told his disciples they was gonna be sheep among wolves, so they hadda be cunning as serpents and look as innocent as doves.

Well, I ain't one to argue with what's in the Bible, so I agreed to Sancho Panza's plan. When a fella's doin' the work of the Lord, ya can't get in his way. Anyhow, I don't suppose Jean Valjean deserves no etiquette. I guess nabbing a fella like that ain't no worse than hogging a buffalo catfish.

*

I STILL HAD THE EMAIL ADDRESS of that Sugar Shack company, so I typed a little message and emailed it to Jean Valjean. I said I was disappointed in him, but that I still wanted him to distribute my dresses. And I said if we was gonna stay partners, we hadda meet face-to-face. I also said personal feelings shouldn't get in the way of business—that's something I got from them Godfather movies, and I thought it sounded real neat. I asked Jean Valjean to join me for lunch at the Bob Evans restaurant in Bowling Green, and I asked him to send me an RSVP if he were agreeable to that.

Now I didn't think nothin' would happen 'cause Jean Valjean don't seem stupid, so I gotta say it surprised me a tad when he instantly answered my email. He said he was really fond of Bob Evans' chicken and collard greens, and he said he would be honored to come to the restaurant and have some lunch with me. So I told him I would meet him on Sunday at noon when I was done with church, and I told him I would be wearing a yellow calico dress.

When Sancho Panza showed up for his afternoon visit, he brought a bag of poppy seed bagels. While we was eatin' the bagels, I told him I would be lunching with Jean Valjean. Sancho Panza he sighed like a furnace and looked at me kinda sad. "Sweet Cosette," he said in a nervous voice, "I'm so sorry to involve you in this. But my soul is so very burdened by the crimes of Jean Valjean."

I told Sancho Panza he don't oughta feel burdened—not if he's doin' God's work. And I said I hoped we could catch some more bluegills after he nabbed Jean Valjean. I said not to worry 'bout bringing no bait 'cause we had plenty of bee moth grubs left.

*

THE FOLLOWING SUNDAY, I drove myself to that Bob Evans restaurant in Bowling Green, and I plopped myself down in one of the booths and waited for Jean Valjean. I had on that yellow calico dress, and I musta looked a fright. It was the same dress Warden Becker gave me when I was freed from Alderson Prison, and that dress is way too big for me and does nothing for my bust. But Bob Evans' restaurants draw crowds after church, so I hadda make sure I stood out. I didn't want Jean Valjean to be overlooking me.

Well, I peeped out the restaurant window, and I didn't see no one approaching. All I saw was Sancho Panza sitting in his black sedan. He was parked on the other side of Three Springs Avenue, and he was chattering away on his cell phone. I ain't sure who he was talking to, but he was chattering like a squirrel.

I was slurpin' a cherry cola, but I hadn't ordered no lunch. Shucks, it woulda been rude to be eating when Jean Valjean arrived. But I hadn't had no breakfast and I was hungrier 'an a bear, and I wished Jean Valjean would show up real quick so I could taste them chicken 'n' collard greens.

Well, my phone it buzzed like a hornet and I held it to my ear, and I felt like a hare in the headlights when I heard Agent Jackson's voice. "Gertie!" he said, and his voice weren't that friendly. "I'm *concerned* about your gay friend. Can you talk on the phone right now? Say nothing if you can't."

Well, talking ain't no problem with me—I'm pretty good at that. It don't take hardly nothin' to start me chatting up a storm.

55

So I asked Agent Jackson if he knew who Cain married when he went to the Land of Nod.

"Young lady," said Agent Jackson, and his voice was harder than iron. "I'm afraid this isn't the *time* to be talking about something like that."

I suppose Agent Jackson was right about that 'cause I just got outta church. And that ain't a very good time to be picking the Bible apart. So I told Agent Jackson 'bout how I was helping to capture Jean Valjean, and I said that proved I'd figgered out the error of my ways. I also said I was mighty hungry 'cause I didn't have no breakfast, and I'd be ordering some chicken and collard greens once Jean Valjean was hauled off to jail. Shucks, I was even hungry enough to have me some black-eyed peas.

Agent Jackson he interrupted me, and his voice was as sharp as a razor. "Young lady, please stop your chatter," he said. "This isn't what you think. You're mixed up with a drug cartel, and I think you're about to be killed."

I suppose if I'd swallowed a jar of white lightning, I couldn't have felt more flushed. Dern, if I thought I was gonna get zapped, I'd have gussied myself up a bit more. I didn't wanna lie on no coroner's slab in that hideous calico dress.

*

AGENT JACKSON WENT ON to tell me some more about Sancho Panza. He said Sancho Panza weren't his real name—that's a character in *Don Quixote*. He said his real name is Juan Perez, but he uses a whole lotta aliases. He said Mister Perez is part of that cartel that had me distributing them dresses, and the reason he was hanging around me was to find out how much I knew. He also said Mister Perez is paranoid, which I guess means that he's crazy, and his plan to capture Jean Valjean weren't nothing but a sham. He was probably testing me to see if I was willing to work with the police.

"Lordy," said Agent Jackson, "you just put your life in his hands. The only thing you've proven is that you're willing to snitch out the cartel."

Agent Jackson said the cops were on their way, but I hadda get outta that restaurant. So I decided I weren't gonna wait around for Jean Valjean to show up. I guess that was sorta rude, but I'd lost my appetite.

Well, I slapped a dollar onto the table to pay for that cherry cola, but I forgot to leave a tip and I still feel ashamed about that. But I weren't thinking 'bout tipping at all as I elbowed my way past the customers. Shucks, after I jostled a waitress and pushed my way out the back door, I sprinted down the sidewalk so fast I ran outta my Sunday pumps.

Well, I hadn't gone but a coupla blocks when I heard a car beeping behind me. I knew it weren't no cop 'cause a cop woulda chirped the siren. So I weren't surprised when I turned my head and saw that black sedan. It was gliding alongside me like a vulture fixing to land, and Sancho Panza, or whatever his name was, was leaning out the driver's window.

"Chica," he said, "please get into the car."

I was kinda glad the fella said please 'cause he was holding a gun in his hand. It was a Smith and Wesson Magnum like the one Pa used to have. And the fella musta just cleaned it 'cause his hands were as dirty as smoke.

I got into the passenger seat and buckled the seat belt quick, 'cause the way he started driving mighta caused an accident. The fella he didn't say nothin', he just merged onto Route 231, and then he started dodging cars like he was trying to outrun the Devil. I started to feel kinda sorry for him 'cause he seemed to be really tormented, so I started a conversation to maybe settle him down.

"If my life is in your hands," I said, "you oughta give 'em a scrub."

The fella he kept his eyes on the road and he handed me the gun, and the gun was so thick with grease that it almost slipped outta my hand. Well, I've cleaned a whole lotta guns in my time and I never saw one so messy, so I pulled a handkerchief outta my purse and wiped it down real good. By the time I finished polishing the gun, I noticed the car had stopped. We was parked in front of a Greyhound Bus Station, and the fella was looking at me.

"Little chica," he said in a voice so warm it coulda heated up soup. "I swear I would never have dirtied my hands if it were not for the Church. Because of the Church, I am going to hell with the mark of Cain on my head."

"I can't believe you're a hitman," I said, and I gave him back the gun.

Well, the fella he uncocked the safety and he patted me on the knee, then he took my handkerchief from me and wiped the grit from his hands. "What I cannot believe, little chica," he said, "is that I could love you so much."

The fella reached into his pocket and he opened up his wallet, and he gave me what musta been two hundred dollars in twenty-dollar bills. "If I do not kill you," he muttered, "others will come for us both. Please get on a bus, Cosette—quickly. Get as far from here as you can."

"Are ya still gonna catch Jean Valjean?" I said 'cause that rascal was still on the loose.

The fella said, "Chica, do not be naïve—please get on a bus. Forget about what's in the Bible, but say a prayer for Jean Valjean."

Well, I took the money from him and he made the sign of the cross, and I gave him a kiss on the neck and didn't say nothing more. I got outta the car and I walked towards the bus station, and the gravel bit into my feet. And that fella he waited 'til I was inside the bus station, 'cause that fella is really thorough. It weren't 'til I bought my ticket that I heard the crack of that Smith and Wesson. There weren't no way to mistake it 'cause them guns make a powerful sound.

*

I'M LIVING IN San Francisco now, and I'm staying in Chinatown. Agent Jackson he pulled some strings to get me into the Witness Protection Program, and he said that no one will look for me in a place like Chinatown. He also asked me to pick a new name so I could change my identity. I was kinda tempted to pick Cosette, but I decided on Ruby Mae.

San Francisco is foggy and fulla bums, but it ain't bad in Chinatown. I'm working in one of them tourist shops that sell stuff that's made in Hong Kong. When I ain't selling knick-knacks, I spend most of my time in a ping-pong parlor on Washington Street. I played a lotta ping-pong when I was a girl, and folks say I'm a natural, so if I practice real hard, I could probably become the ping-pong champion of Chinatown.

I miss Sancho Panza real bad and I hope he ain't met the Devil, 'cause the Church says folks who bump 'emselves off are gonna end up in hell. But, wherever he is, I hope he found out just who Cain went and married. I ain't figgered out the answer myself, but other things are coming my way. In San Francisco, it shouldn't be long 'til I find me another gay friend.

The food's real good in Chinatown and the restaurants are getting to know me, and I always show my appreciation by leaving a three-dollar tip. I especially like the dim sum and the sweet 'n' sour pork. Still, there's times I wish I could find a place that'll serve me some black-eyed peas.

6. The Ping-Pong Champion of Chinatown

WELL, IT'S ME AGAIN, Gertie McDowell. I'm still in the Witness Protection Program and hiding out in Chinatown, and I'm still working part-time in that souvenir shop and playing a whole lot of ping-pong. And if you've read this far, we're probably good friends and you'll wanna know more about me. So I'm gonna tell ya what happened to me after I'd been in San Francisco two months.

I'm gonna start out my story real slow 'cause things get crazy fast. So I'm gonna start on this day I was strolling along Pier 39. The bay was kinda choppy and the sea lions were barkin' like dogs and the fog was so bright and cottony, I could hardly see Alcatraz. So I started to think 'bout the Bible again 'cause fog does that to me. I wondered if Jesus went too far when he raised Lazarus from the dead. The Bible only mentions that in the Gospel According to John, so I'm guessing that Jesus overdid it when he woke up Lazarus. Shucks, Lazarus was probably in heaven strummin' on a harp, and he probably didn't appreciate it when Jesus brought him back.

I called the Nose on my cell phone—I still call him pretty regular—and I asked him what he thought about Lazarus getting raised from the dead. The Nose he got kinda snippy 'cause he's tired of my Bible questions, and he said I don't need to think about nothin' but picking up worms with my toes. He said as far as Lazarus goes, he mighta been in hell, and Jesus mighta done him a favor when he took him outta there. Well, that don't make no sense neither, and I told that to the Nose. I said that if Lazarus went to hell, maybe Jesus shoulda left him there. Maybe Jesus shouldn't have released no wicked man upon the world. The Nose he got even snippier and told me to drop the subject. He said not to bother him again about stuff as stupid as that. He said not to call him unless I was willing to be filmed dangling worms from my toes.

Well, I caught a bus back to Chinatown 'cause the Bible was giving me a headache. And I went to the ping-pong parlor on Washington Street to find myself a match. I'm better than ever at ping-pong 'cause I'm training to be a champion, but that ain't why I went there that particular afternoon. I went there 'cause ya don't gotta think about nothing when you're slamming that ball back and forth.

*

WELL, YA AIN'T GONNA BELIEVE who I ran into when I went into that ping-pong parlor. At first, I didn't recognize him 'cause he was dressed up like a woman. He had on a big ol' maxi dress and he was wearing a shoulder-length wig, but when he looked at me with his lazy eye I realized who he was. I said to him, "Warden Jordan, whatcha doin' in San Francisco?"

Warden Jordan he looked at me like that was a real dumb question. Shucks, when you're a cross-dresser like him, there ain't no place else you can go. He didn't answer my question, he just grinned like a possum with gas. And he said to me, "Sweets, you as good at ping-pong as ya are at playing checkers?"

Well, one of them ping-pong tables was vacant so he challenged me to a match, and I beat him 11-4 without even breaking a sweat. But Warden Jordan was panting like a coon dog after a hunt, and he said he needed to cool down a tad 'cause his heart was about to burst. He offered to buy me a root beer—he said the loser always pays.

We sat ourselves down in the snack bar and Warden Jordan bought us both root beers, and I asked Warden Jordan how he happened to be lying in wait for me. Warden Jordan said he's a detective now at the San Francisco Hall of Justice—it's the only place that would hire him after he was fired from Alderson Prison. He said he was assigned to the Special Victims Unit, which investigates human trafficking, and that's 'cause a gender bender like him ain't likely to attract suspicion. The warden showed me his detective badge, which was tucked behind his bra, and said it ain't hard to work undercover when you blend right into the city.

The warden said he suspected he'd find me here 'cause he's got a lotta snitches, and one of 'em told him this hick girl in Chinatown was putting on all kinds of airs. His snitch told him this girl was training to be the ping-pong champion of Chinatown. "Sweets," said Warden Jordan, and he gave me a rattlesnake grin. "I said to myself only Gertie McDowell would aspire to something like that."

When I told him my name was Ruby Mae now, the warden just blew his nose. He said whatever my name was, it was time for another bet. He said if I could beat him two games outta three he would buy me some Birkenstock sandals. And he said if he won the next two games, I would have to do him a favor.

Well, golly, that weren't no wager at all—I'd already powdered him once. So I told Warden Jordan he had him a bet 'cause I needed a new pair of sandals. I didn't even bother to ask him what the favor was—I figgered it didn't matter since he didn't have no chance.

We played another game, and the warden he nipped me 22-20. The reason the score was so high is 'cause ya gotta win by two points. So we had us a real lively game, and both of us made some great shots. And while we was playing, a great big crowd gathered 'round the table. Fifty or sixty people was cheerin' us on in Chinese.

The crowd it didn't go nowhere when we started our final game, and I played Warden Jordan six feet from the table so's to handle his spins and his slams. I practically had to play him by ear—the ball was comin' that fast—and when the game was over the warden had beat me 23-21.

Well, the spectators gave a great big cheer after the warden hit the winning shot, and a coupla of 'em said that was one of the finest contests they had ever seen. But I weren't thinking too much about that 'cause I was feeling as dumb as a goose. Shucks, I had just been hustled by that crazy Warden Jordan.

*

WARDEN JORDAN HE drove me to Fisherman's Warf, and he said he was buying me lunch. He said that this time the loser weren't gonna have to pay. Well, I figgered he wanted a really big favor, and I may as well have something special. So I ordered me one of them chowders that are served inside a bread bowl—that's gotta be one of the fanciest meals that I have ever seen. 'Cause once you're done eating your chowder, you can wolf down the bowl as well. And the best thing about it is that you don't even gotta stop to sop your bread.

Warden Jordan he didn't eat nothin', he just gave me a mushy look. I guess the fog hiding Alcatraz was making him sentimental. He looked at me real tender and he patted me on the hand, and he said to me, "Gertie, I have to say you were always my favorite girl."

I said, "If I was your favorite girl, the rest musta had it *real* bad."

Warden Jordan said, "Being my favorite girl doesn't give you immunity. I'm still going to collect that favor that I won from you fair and square."

I said to Warden Jordan, "I ain't sure it was won fair and square. I didn't think you could play ping-pong while wearing a maxi dress."

Warden Jordan he told me to finish my lunch and don't take too long about it. He said he don't like discussing business while folks is slurping down chowder. So I finished eating the chowder and I gobbled up the bread bowl, and I asked Warden Jordan what he thought about Jesus raising Lazarus from the dead. Warden Jordan said it don't hurt a body to get itself resurrected. He said that he was proof of that, and he thanked me for making that dress. He also said that was beside the point, and it was time to discuss that favor.

Now there's things you don't expect to hear when folks is wanting a favor. You think maybe they'll want you to feed their dog while they're attending a turkey shoot—or maybe they'll want you to help catch a pig that wandered into a church. What you don't expect 'em to ask you is to break up a white slavery ring, but that's what Warden Jordan said he wanted me to do. He said young ladies were answering internet ads to get work modeling dresses, and these girls were getting kidnapped instead and auctioned to local brothels. He told me I could help him out by responding to one of them ads, 'cause them auction houses were hid in back alleys and hard for the police to find. He said only girls that look really naïve could infiltrate them auction houses, and if I succeeded in getting kidnapped, I was to memorize the address. He promised that after I texted him and gave him the location, the cops would raid the auction house and put them slavers in jail.

Well, that weren't too big a favor to ask in exchange for a bread bowl chowder. White slavery it don't seem no worse to me than being married to Benny Pearman. So I told Warden Jordan I'd do him that favor as long as he didn't want nothin' else. I said, after the cops put them slavers in jail, he could buy me some Peking duck.

*

AFTER I CHATTED with Warden Jordan, I took a bus back to the ping-pong parlor. 'Cause if someone wearing a maxi dress could beat me two games outta three, it didn't seem too likely that I was gonna become no champion. Not unless I had me some practice time and got some mustard on my serve. And speakin' 'bout mustard, that got me to thinking 'bout Jesus feedin' the masses—'bout how he blessed a few fishes and loaves, and that fed five thousand people. That miracle kinda bothers me 'cause it don't seem particularly fair. Not everyone is fond of fish, ya know, so some of the crowd musta stayed hungry. I think Jesus shoulda blessed some hotdogs as well and maybe some collard greens.

While I was sittin' on the bus, I phoned the Nose 'cause I wanted his opinion. And I asked him if Jesus was playing fair when he only blessed fishes and loaves. The Nose said I gotta quit bothering him with such idiotic questions, and unless I had something more to tell him, he was gonna hang up his phone. So I told the Nose how I met Warden Jordan and how he suckered me, and how I now hadda help him break up a white slavery ring.

The Nose he said I don't oughta team up with a fella like Warden Jordan. He said the police don't got no interest in busting up prostitution, and Warden Jordan's a fool if he thinks that's ever gonna happen. The Nose told me he used to be a pimp before he started his foot fetish site, and he said he never had no trouble paying off the cops.

Well, I thanked the Nose for his opinion 'bout fellas like Warden Jordan. But I said I also wanted his thoughts about Jesus blessing hotdogs. The Nose said that Jesus couldn't 'a' blessed hotdogs 'cause they didn't have none in his day. He said the only things left for Jesus to bless were goat cheese and matzo ball soup.

*

WELL, THE PING-PONG TOURNAMENT was starting when I went into the parlor, so it didn't look like I'd have no chance for practice time. I was seeded fourth outta sixteen players, which gave me an easy first match. My first-round opponent was a fella that looked 'bout a hundred years old, and that fella was real indignant 'cause he didn't wanna play no woman. Well, I didn't wanna act like no feminist, so I took it kinda easy on him. I let him win half a dozen points before beatin' him 11-6, 11-0.

In the second round, I played this kid who was nothin' but elbows and knees. And he weren't too hard to beat neither 'cause he kept looking at my tits. Shucks, the first rule of playin' ping-pong is to keep your eye on the ball, and this kid he watched for my tits to jiggle every time I returned a shot. Well, my bust it ain't nothin' to brag about and I don't think it jiggled much, so the kid lost the match for nothin' when I clobbered him 11-2. 11-1.

While I was waitin' to play in the semi-finals, I got a text message. The message was from Warden Jordan, and it was kinda long. He told me to show up at Clay Street and Kearny at the edge of Chinatown, 'cause that's where the slavers were picking up girls and hauling 'em off to sell. He said he had answered the ad in my name and to be there by 6:00 p.m. He also told me that stupid ad was written in Chinese, so I hadda convince them slavers that I had some Oriental blood. He said to wear a kimono so's to make sure they snatched me up.

Well, it was already 4:30 p.m. and tournament weren't done for the day, and I didn't wanna get kidnapped by slavers before winning my semi-final match. But the fella I was scheduled to play he had an accident. The moment our match began, he turned his ankle real bad. Shucks, I could hear it crackle like popcorn as soon as he served me the ball. When the paramedics carried him out on a stretcher, he was crying like a lamb, so I advanced to the championship round without even smacking a ball.

*

THE CHAMPIONSHIP GAME weren't scheduled 'til 2:00 p.m. the next day, and that gave me time to get myself kidnapped and bust up the white slavery ring. So I walked two miles to Japantown to buy me a kimono, and I found one in a second-hand clothing store on Geary Boulevard. The kimono was pretty short and it showed off my legs real nice, and my thighs are really shapely 'cause of all the farm work I done. So I stuffed my dress into a shopping bag and I put on the kimono, and I knew I was gonna look my best when them slavers snatched me up.

Well, it was gettin' close to 6:00 p.m. so I flagged me down a cab, and I told the driver to take me to the corner of Clay Street and Kearny. And on the way there, I started thinking 'bout what I was doin'. And the more I thought about what I was doin', the more it didn't make no sense. So I called up Agent Jackson 'cause I wanted a second opinion, and I hadda leave a voice message 'cause he didn't answer my call. But I guess I already knew what Agent Jackson was gonna tell me. He'd have probably said that I got a bad habit of letting folks lead me astray, but that no one oughta be led astray by a fella like Warden Jordan. And I'll bet he'd have said that Warden Jordan was probably just a showboat, and that he was out to impress the mayor so's to get himself a promotion. And I guess he woulda also reminded me that I was in the

Witness Protection Program, and a person who was under federal protection oughtn't be trying to get kidnapped. All this made a lot of sense, but I couldn't wrap my head around it. 'Cause gettin' kidnapped didn't seem worse than welching on a bet.

These thoughts were still bouncing around in my head when I got out at Clay Street and Kearny, and, on top of that, I was hungry after playing them ping-pong matches. So I bought a hotdog from a street vendor 'cause hotdogs settle me down. I smeared the hotdog with mustard and I nibbled it real slow, and I was hopin' that maybe them slavers weren't gonna show up after all. But it weren't but a minute later that this car pulled up alongside me.

*

THE CAR HAD NO ONE in it but this ratty looking fella. His face was scarred from acne and he had buck teeth like a rodent, and he rolled down the passenger side window and started talking to me in Chinese. I couldn't tell what he was saying, so I just nodded and said, "Ah so" 'cause I think that's what you're supposed to say when you're dressed in a kimono. The fella he made this motion for me to get into the car, so I finished eating my hotdog then slipped into the seat beside him.

Well, the fella he didn't say nothing as we pulled away from the curb. He just started driving real cautious and checking his rearview mirror. After we'd gone a dozen blocks and made a whole buncha turns, he parked in front of a laundromat and looked at me kinda suspicious.

"You wan be model?" he said to me in a voice fulla disbelief. Well, I didn't wanna tell him no lie 'cause that wouldn't 'a' been polite, so I told him what I wanted to be was the ping-pong champion of Chinatown.

The fella he kept looking at me then a light came into his eyes. "Ah-ha!" he said. "But you famous already. You Liddle Miss Twinkle Toes."

Well, I told him my feet were retired and my name was now Ruby Mae, and I said I was trying to pick up a few bucks by working as a model.

"No madda," the fella said with a smirk. "You gonna fetch top dolla."

Well, there's things a girl don't expect to happen when she's getting nabbed by a slaver, and one of 'em is that she's gonna get asked to autograph a ping-pong paddle. But the fella handed me a ping-pong paddle, and he asked me to sign the handle. "No sign it Ruby Mae," he said. "Sign Liddle Miss Twinkle Toes."

When he shoved a pencil into my hand, I felt like writing something rude. But I scratched my stage name onto the handle and I gave him back his paddle, and the fella he looked so grateful that I felt a bit ashamed. Shucks, just 'cause I once was a video star, don't mean I can rant like Charlie Sheen.

The fella he bowed then invited me to get into the back of the car. "You Liddle Miss Twinkle Toes," he said. "You no godda ride in front."

Well, I slipped into the back seat of the car as he held the door open for me, and he said it would make him real happy if I would pose for a photo with him. So the fella he sat beside me and snapped a selfie of us both, then he got back into the driver's seat and we pulled away from the curb.

We cruised down Jackson Street for a while and we made a couple turns, then we pulled into an alley that was darker than a tomb. The building we stopped in front of looked like an abandoned warehouse, and the only thing that lit it up was a light from a dentist's office. The office it had a neon sign that spelled out Dr. Tong.

Well, the fella he parked in front of the warehouse and started to chat on his cell phone, so I whipped my own phone outta my bra and texted Warden Jordan. I couldn't make out the name of the street—I ain't even sure it had one. But I'm real good in an emergency, and I did the next best thing.

It's next to Dr. Tong, I typed then I hit the send arrow quick.

*

THE FELLA HE TOOK ME by the arm and he hustled me through a side door, and the next thing I knew I was standing on a stage with ten or twelve Chinese girls. A group of seedy looking men was crowded around the stage, and they was puffing on hookahs and bidding on the girls. And the girls was wearing ankle chains and some of 'em was crying, and this skinny little fella with a booming voice was auctioning 'em off one by one.

Well, a couple of slavers greeted me then fitted me with ankle chains, and one of 'em made me open my mouth so he could inspect my teeth. I bit that fella's finger 'cause that got me real upset, and that fella he yelped like a bee-stung dog and the whole crowd started to laugh.

A moment later, the fella I bit yanked off both of my sneakers, and the auctioneer he pointed at me and started jabbering like a jay. I couldn't tell what he was saying 'cause he was yakking in Chinese, but then I heard him yell out, "Liddle Miss Twinkle Toes!"

The crowd it gave a cheer so loud my eardrums started buzzing—I could tell them folks were really eager to put a price on me. But the auctioneer he made them wait—I guess he wanted to build anticipation. Shucks, I was hoping to get auctioned off quick 'cause I hadda pee real bad, but the fella he made me stand there while all the other girls were sold off first. It weren't 'til the final girl was sold and led away like a heifer, that I got shoved to the front of the stage, and the crowd started bidding on me.

As I listened to all them bidders trying to outshout each other, I wished the cops would hurry up and haul them off to jail. But suddenly it dawned on me that that weren't gonna happen. I had been there for over an hour, and the police hadn't shown up yet.

*

YA KNOW, I'M STARTIN' to wonder why I'm telling all this stuff. 'Cause there ain't nothin' more shameful than standing in shackles while a crowd is bidding on you. Stuff like that ain't just embarrassin', it's downright scary as well. But just when I thought things couldn't get no worse, the side door opened up, and the creepiest fella I ever seen came slinking into the room. The fella was pale as a maggot and he wore a saffron robe, and he had a long ragged beard that was as black as a raven's wing. He was toting a shopping bag that was probably full of money, and he looked at me like a hungry wolf sizing up a fawn.

The fella he stood at the edge of the crowd and he listened to the bidding, then he walloped his palms together and shouted, "One thousand dolla!" His voice was so deep and hollow that it prickled the skin on my neck—it may as well have been rumbling from the bottom of a well.

The crowd it got real silent, as though someone had fired a gun, and that fella he just scowled like he was daring someone to speak. When a voice shouted "two thousand dolla," the fella puffed up like a toad—he appeared to be a person who was accustomed to getting his way. Well, he elbowed his way to the front of the crowd and looked the auctioneer right in the eye, and he bellowed "TEN THOUSAND DOLLA!" and that settled all arguments. The fella gave his shopping bag to the skinny auctioneer, and the auctioneer turned the bag over and a lotta hundred dollar bills fell out.

Well, the auctioneer counted the money then he handed some of it back—I guess 'cause it wouldn't be honest to accept more than the price that was bid. But the fella who bought me waved him away and said something in Chinese, and a coupla slavers unlocked my shackles and turned me over to him.

*

AFTER THAT FELLA BOUGHT ME, he slapped a dog collar 'round my neck then he hooked a leash to the collar and led me outta the warehouse. Once we was out in the alley, I told him I hadda pee bad, and the fella said, "Do it quickly, my dear" and his voice sounded real familiar. I squatted behind a dumpster while the fella held onto the leash, and he turned his head away from me while I relieved myself. I gotta say this about him, that dude was a gentleman.

"Quickly, my dear," the fella repeated. "We have to get out of here."

He tugged on the leash real gentle, like I was a champion broodmare, and he led me to this Chrysler that had a rental car plate on the back. Next thing I know, I was sittin' in the Chrysler while the dude kept hold of the leash, and we was driving all over the city in no particular direction. We drove through the Financial District and we drove through the Tenderloin and we drove past the Hall of Justice where Warden Jordan works. We even drove past Golden Gate Park and we skirted the Richmond District, and we doubled back and passed that store in Japantown where I picked up my kimono. By the time the fella parked the car we was sittin' in Twin Peaks Park, and the city was glittering below us like fireflies frozen in flight.

The fella he unhooked the leash from my collar, and he looked at me kinda woeful like maybe he weren't particularly thrilled about buying a video star. As he took the collar offa my neck, his hands trembled like wounded pigeons. "Honey," he said in a voice fulla gloom, "we have come to the end of our road."

Dern, if his voice weren't familiar as sin, but I didn't recognize his face at all. Not 'til he pulled off his raggedy beard, which he musta bought in a costume store. Maybe ya already knew who it was, but it came as a surprise to me. Shucks, I gaped like a baby bird when I saw it was the Nose.

*

I REMEMBERED HOW the Nose once said I was gonna walk among stars. That never exactly happened, but I ain't gonna fault him none. 'Cause lookin' at the lights of San Francisco came purty close to that.

The Nose told me that right after I phoned him, he hopped on a flight from L.A. He said he figgered it wouldn't be long until I was in trouble deep.

"Howja know where to find me?" I asked.

The Nose he rubbed his eyes. "My muse, my love, my heart," he said, "remember I once was a pimp. A pimp can sniff out white slavery much quicker than a cop."

Well, I felt like I'd won me a lottery, but my feet were still retired. So I told the Nose I weren't posing for his videos even though he just purchased me. Not unless he could show me a legal bill of sale.

The Nose he confessed that he had reformed—that he didn't film feet no more. But he didn't seem too happy about it, he just sat there rubbing his eyes. He said all the joy had been sucked from his life, and he was wandering in darkness now. He said his muse had cast him adrift, and he was only a shell of a man.

Well, I thanked the Nose for buying me, and the Nose just bowed his head. He said it was only money and money was so overrated. He said he would give every penny he had to recover his passion for feet.

I figgered this was a pretty good time to bring up the Bible again. So I asked the Nose if Jesus went too far when he raised Lazarus from the dead. The Nose he took my hand in his, and his face was like melted wax. And he said that Jesus should never have taken Lazarus outta the tomb.

Well, the Nose he started to cry, and I felt really sorry for him. Shucks, I can't remember when I saw somebody so depressed. So I said I was really sorry that he weren't a pervert no more, and I gave him a smooch on the cheek and I slipped outta that rental car. I figgered a fella as sad as the Nose needed time to compose himself.

I walked all the way back to Chinatown, which took me almost two hours. 'Cause walkin' ain't too easy when you don't got shoes on your feet.

*

AGENT JACKSON he called me the following morning and said he got my message. And when I told him what happened, he said the Nose oughta get a medal. He said Warden Jordan musta dropped the ball, but that didn't matter too much. 'Cause the feds had a plan to round up them slavers for violating the Mann Act. Agent Jackson said it was nice talking to me and to not get into no more trouble. And he said he was looking forward to having some coffee with me.

That afternoon, I returned to the ping-pong parlor to play the championship match. I hadda play in an old pair of sandals since them slavers took my sneakers. The fella I played was rangy and fast, but he didn't give me too much trouble. We was playing the best outta five, but I only hadda play three games. I beat the fella 12-10, 12-10, and 11-9. The crowd it gave me a great big cheer and folks patted me on the back, and they said it was the first time a woman won the ping-pong championship.

The trophy they gave me was made outta plastic and was only six inches high, and the prize weren't nothin' but a discount coupon for the Golden Gate Bakery. And when I checked the San Francisco Chronicle the next day, I saw nothin' but baseball scores—the paper hadn't taken the space to mention me at all. But my heart was as light as a bubble, and I felt like putting on airs. On Washington Street, I would always be known as the ping-pong champion of Chinatown.

7. The Goblins that Getcha

I HOPE THE TIME I spent with them slavers didn't lower your opinion of me. If it did, the story I'm about to tell you ain't gonna improve it none. But at least it's got some romance in it, and that oughta soften things up. Ya know, folks will let almost anything slide if you give 'em a bit of romance.

It had been a coupla weeks since the Nose saved me from them slavers, and for a while, it looked like things was getting back to normal. Or 'bout as normal as things can get if ya live in San Francisco. I read in the paper the other day that the FBI busted them rascals and locked 'em up in the Hall of Justice where Warden Jordan works. And the mayor he came on television and said slavers are lowlife scum, and there ain't no hole in the city deep enough for their kind to hide in. And Agent Jackson he phoned me the day after them slavers were busted, and he said the day was comin' when he would have coffee with me.

Well, it didn't take too long for things to get rowdy again, so I'm gonna start this story out at a time when I was fulla repose. After working my shift at Ying's Bazar, I took the bus to Muir Woods, and I was walking among the redwoods and thinking some really deep thoughts. There ain't nothin' like towering redwoods to make a girl get thoughtful—I'll bet some of 'em trees date all the way back to the days of Richard Nixon. I was thinking back to when I was sixteen and still living in Turkey Roost, and how one day Father Daugherty asked me to chase some pigs outta the church. It was an especially scorching summer and them pigs were baking outdoors, so them oinkers kept sneaking into the church so they could lie on the cool wooden floor. Well, I helped Father Daugherty chase them pigs from the church, but later I got to thinking. I got to wonderin' if it were Christian to force them pigs outta God's house. See, the townsfolk they only needed the church for a coupla hours on Sunday, but them pigs was baking like cakes on a griddle and needed it all the time. So I phoned the Nose and asked him if what I done was right. I asked him if it was Christian of me to shoo them pigs from the church.

Well, the Nose he's been testier 'an ever since he gave up filming feet, and he told me I hadda stop bothering him with questions that don't make no sense. He told me to find something better to do than bug him all the time, and he said I was making him regret that he bought me from them slavers. But then the Nose got to thinking and his voice got a whole lot softer, and he said the church oughta open its doors to them that needs it most.

I ain't sure what the Nose meant by that, and I got even more confused. But I thanked him for his opinion, and I told him to have a good day. And then I jumped on the shuttle bus and went back to Chinatown.

*

AFTER I GOT BACK to Chinatown, I went to the ping-pong parlor. Heck, every time I go there, I get pampered like royalty. No matter that I may have sinned when I shooed them pigs outta the church—in that ping-pong parlor on Washington Street, I'm treated like a queen.

Well, I walked into the ping-pong parlor and Warden Jordan was there, and for a moment I started wondering if my sins were catching up to me. 'Cause the warden he was wearing a dark black funeral-type dress, and I could tell by his sour expression that he had unfinished business with me. He was holding a ping-pong paddle and bouncing a ball offa it, and that ball was hopping as rapid as a toad in a frying pan.

"Sweets," said Warden Jordan, and he kept on bouncing that ball. "I really don't want to believe what my ears have been telling me."

"What have yer ears been tellin' you?" I said to Warden Jordan.

"That you have the nerve to call yourself a ping-pong champion."

"Shucks," I said to Warden Jordan. "All of Chinatown is calling me that. So I guess the whole of Chinatown has got a lot of nerve."

Warden Jordan he grabbed the ball outta the air like he was snatchin' himself a fly. "It's dangerous to have too much nerve," he said, and he crushed the ball in his fist. "But things are gonna get saner when I take you down a peg."

Well, it seemed that Warden Jordan had come to take my title away, and I was feeling out-of-sorts enough to let him have a try. 'Cause Warden Jordan never came to my rescue when I was being auctioned to them brothel owners. And nothin' will rile a girl up more than getting sold to a brothel.

Well, we chose ourselves a ping-pong table and we played the best outta three, and all the warden wanted to do was smash the ball real hard. So I played him eight feet away from the table so I could return his smashes, and every time he walloped the ball I hit him a real high lob. Well, it weren't too long 'til he started missing the table or smashing the ball into the net, so I just kept feeding him lobs so's to let him beat himself. I think that funeral dress he was wearing made it hard to stretch for the ball, 'cause it took me less than an hour to hang onto my championship. I won by scores of 11-6 and 19-17.

The warden's mood was sour before we started the match, and it got a whole lot worse after I walloped him. He bought me another root beer 'cause the loser gotta pay, and then he told me the police department had put him on administrative leave. He said he was under investigation and would probably lose his job 'cause his plan to bust them slavers it didn't go too well. He asked me why I texted him a location he couldn't find. "Miss McDowell," he said in a voice that could pickle a shoat, "do you know how many Dr. Tongs there are in Chinatown?"

I said that was like asking me if pigs belong in a church, and I said there ain't a whole lot of sense in bringing up subjects like that. Warden Jordan said there ain't much sense in my being in the Witness Protection Program, not if I was running around puttin' on airs and attracting a whole lot of attention. I asked Warden Jordan how he knew I was in the Witness Protection Program, and Warden Jordan he told me that he had a buncha sources.

Well, Warden Jordan he finished his root beer, and then he ruffled my hair. And he said, "Gertie, you'd better remember that winning streaks come to an end." He didn't say nothin' more, he just walked outta the ping-pong parlor, and I felt like something was coming my way that weren't too agreeable.

A few seconds later, this big ol' crow flew into the ping-pong parlor. It was a really elegant bird with feathers that gleamed like wet tar, and it perched itself right on the table where I skunked Warden Jordan. The crow didn't caw or flap its wings, it just stood there looking around, and I remembered something Ma told me before she went into the nursing home. She said when a crow comes a calling, death ain't far behind.

*

WHEN I WAS A GIRL, Ma recited a poem so's to get me to behave. It was written by James Whitcomb Riley, and it's called "Little Orphan Annie." Orphan Annie was a maid who told stories 'bout witches and goblins, and she told some kids that goblins would get 'em if they didn't obey God's laws. Ma recited that poem 'cause she knew I been smoking and stealing apples from Widder Brown's orchard, and she said it was just a matter of time 'til them goblins snatched me up. Well, after I turned twenty last year, I told Ma that I ain't seen no goblins, and I said it looked like my sins weren't bad enough to bring them boogers around. Ma said that's just 'cause them goblins were busy snatching moonshiners and politicians, but it wouldn't be much longer 'til they got around to me. She said she knew how I went to Los Angeles and posed for some perv called the Nose, and she said that kinda depravity oughta hurry them goblins up.

Well, after I saw Warden Jordan, I had me a goblin-type dream. I was living back in Turkey Roost and my Jeep just wouldn't start, so I went to Willie's Salvage Yard to buy myself a starter. Willie he weren't around, which I thought was pretty unusual. I ain't never been to Willie's Salvage Yard and not seen Willie there. Willie he's all the time stripping cars and selling fuel filters and carburetors, and if you're on your way to Miller's Pond, he'll sell you blood worms too. Well, I went into Willie's Salvage Yard and looked around for him, but all I saw was some stringy fella with eyebrows like wooly worms. Well, everyone knows that wooly worms mean winter's bearing down, and the fella seemed aware of that as he stood there looking at me. The fella said he owned the salvage yard 'cause Willie done sold it to him, and he told me his name was Charlie Cheap but I could call him the Muffler Man. Well, I said to the dude I ain't calling him nothin' 'cause I didn't know him from Adam, and he said everyone knows him sooner or later and I oughta be more polite. Well, that fella's nose changed into a beak then he started to caw like a crow, so I figgered that someone as ill-bred as that don't deserve no politeness at all. I said I weren't buying none of his mufflers and I walked outta the salvage yard, and all the time I was walking away, he kept cawing like a crow.

When I woke up, I was kinda upset 'cause rudeness does that to me. So I called up Agent Jackson and I told him 'bout my dream, and I said that muffler fella didn't have no manners at all. Agent Jackson said my dream might be a bad omen, and I oughta start being more careful. He suggested I change my address now and then and quit entering ping-pong tournaments, and he advised me to have nothin' further to do with that crazy Warden Jordan. He also told me he was on his way to San Francisco to testify in a case, and he said if I had some time to spare he would like to have coffee with me.

*

A COUPLE OF DAYS LATER, I made a date to have coffee with Agent Jackson. I asked him to meet me in Golden Gate Bakery 'cause I still had that discount coupon. I wanted to get us some custard tarts 'cause tarts go well with coffee, and the Golden Gate Bakery is famous for its creamy custard tarts. I asked him to meet me there at eight in the morning, 'cause that's when the tarts are fresh.

Well, the bakery was crowded when I got there so I hadda wait to be seated, but that was okay 'cause Agent Jackson showed up an hour late. When he finally walked into the bakery, I almost didn't recognize him. He looked really tired and he walked with a limp, and the frost on his temples was thicker. I guess jailing all them drug dealers was taking it out of him. But my heart hopped like a duck on a June bug when he gave me a friendly wave, then he came to my table and shook my hand and said, "How are you doing, Gertie?"

I could smell a trace of likker on him, and that surprised me a tad. I never thought for a moment that he was a drinking man. But, shucks, that didn't bother me none 'cause his manners were still real nice. 'Sides, a good woman's love is all a man needs to cure him of a drinking habit.

I asked him how his daughters were doing, and he said they were doing fine, and he said he wished he could see 'em more but his work was getting in the way. He asked me if I had gotten over my experience of getting kidnapped, and I told him them slavers were a lot less annoying than Benny Pearman was. I asked him if he wanted a custard tart and he said that sounded tempting, so I used my discount coupon to fetch us a coupla custard tarts. And then I asked him what he took with his coffee and he said he liked half-and-half, and I told him I liked it with half-and-half too and I fixed us a coupla cups.

Well, we sat for about an hour and chatted like old friends, and things didn't seem no different from when I seen him last. 'Cept that his hand was shaking when he held his coffee cup and, after a while, he reached in his jacket and pulled out a flask of likker. He poured a dollop of likker into his coffee cup, and I could tell from the way he was blushing that he felt kinda bad about that. But, shucks, I didn't pay that no mind 'cause his face had the hue of a rose. And after he finished his coffee, his hand was steadier 'an a post.

Well, Agent Jackson he told me he had the whole day off, and he asked me if I would like to see some of the city with him. I told him I had no other commitments so he flagged us down a cab, and he had the driver drop us off at an entrance to Golden Gate Park. When we got into the park, we took us a stroll through the Japanese Tea Garden, and I could see buncha golden carp stirring beneath the lily pads. The Garden was fulla paths and bridges and statues of Japanese gods, and a couple of homeless people were sleeping under a manicured bush. I told Agent Jackson I had a kimono that I bought to fool them slavers, and I told him I'd have worn it if I knew we was coming here.

After a while, we sat down on a bench and watched some geese picking up bugs, and Agent Jackson he said he was grateful to have my company. Well, I told Agent Jackson to not be so grateful 'cause I had a confession to make, and I told him how the Nose took all them videos of my feet. I also mentioned how the Nose posted them videos on his internet site, and that I was known among perverts as Little Miss Twinkle Toes. I didn't wanna tell Agent Jackson this stuff, but a girl has gotta be honest. Heck, I don't wanna spend no time with a man that I gotta keep secrets from.

Agent Jackson he didn't say nothin', he just sat there stroking his jaw. And I told him I wouldn't blame him none if he didn't wanna see me no more. After a while, Agent Jackson said he was glad I was honest with him. He said what I done was foolish, but that I was still a very nice girl. He said that it looked like maybe I needed someone looking after me.

Agent Jackson decided he owed me a lunch 'cause I'd bought him a custard tart. He took me to this big ol' museum that has a restaurant in it, and he held the door open for me as we walked into the museum. I had me a burger and a double order of fries 'cause I was hungrier 'an a hound, and Agent Jackson had him a bowl of chili that he ate with sourdough bread. And when we was done with our lunch, we took a stroll around this lake, and the lake was fulla paddleboats and the water was churning with carp. Well, I was feeling kinda chilly 'cause the sun was goin' down, and Agent Jackson musta seen I was shivering 'cause he put his jacket over my shoulders. He asked if I would like to go to his hotel for some more conversation and coffee, and I told him I couldn't have sex with him 'cause I was having my period.

Agent Jackson he laughed and said he weren't expecting no sex, and I told him I was really glad he was such a gentleman. Ya know, I ain't never had sex with no one 'cept for Benny Pearman, and that was only 'cause I hadda perform my wifely duty. Benny he never took longer 'an a minute, and that was fine with me.

Agent Jackson he caught us another cab, and we went to his hotel. He was staying at the Fairmont, which is close to Union Square, and I let him hold my hand as we rode the elevator up to his room. I hope that didn't make me no hussy, but I liked him holding my hand.

When we got to Agent Jackson's room, we sat on this big double couch, and he ordered some coffee for us and I poured us a coupla cups. I fixed our coffee with lotsa cream, but Agent Jackson preferred to drink scotch, and he poured himself a glassful and we talked through mosta the night. I talked 'bout hoggin' catfish in the criks near Turkey Roost, and how ya hadda be careful so as not to get stuck by the spines. And Agent Jackson told me about busting up drug cartels and how he got shot in his leg. That happened several months ago and he hadda be hospitalized, and it took him a while to recuperate or he'd have come to see me sooner.

We talked 'til I couldn't talk no more 'cause my eyes got heavy with sleep, and Agent Jackson said I could have his bed and he would take the couch. I told him I wouldn't hear of that 'cause I wanted to sleep beside him, and I snuggled up right next to him when we stretched out on the bed. I felt as pleased as a pig in mud as I slept beside Agent Jackson. I never felt more protected even though he was a little bit drunk.

*

WHILE I WAS SLEEPING BESIDE Agent Jackson, I had another goblin dream. In my dream, the city of San Francisco had planned a parade for me. That's 'cause I had just become the ping-pong champion of Chinatown. Well, I was waiting for a limousine to fetch me and drive me up Market Street, and I could see hundreds of people lining the street so they could wave at me. And then this hearse pulled up alongside me and the driver looked outta the window, and the driver was that same ornery fella I met in the salvage yard. He had them same bushy eyebrows and his fingers were thin as bloodworms, and he told me to get my butt into the hearse 'cause my future was calling me. Well, I asked him who he thought he was to be picking me up in a hearse, and he said his name was Charlie Cheap but I could call him the Muffler Man. I told him I weren't calling him nothin' but a stalker and a creep, and that if he wanted to accommodate me he could not turn into no crow. The fella he said there comes a time when everyone rides with him, and he said he would come back and fetch me when I was feeling more neighborly. And the fella he pulled away from the curb and he drove up Market Street, and I didn't feel nothin' but glad when I couldn't see his car no more.

Well, I told Agent Jackson 'bout my dream while we was having breakfast. We was sitting in the dining room where they have a smorgasbord. Agent Jackson he said the dream might be a warning that someone was after me. He told me to keep a low profile and to not be attracting attention, and he told me to stay outta Chinatown 'cause too many folks know me there. Agent Jackson said he had business to do inside the Federal Building, and he asked me to meet him at 6:00 p.m. by the fountain in Yerba Buena Gardens. He said that's a real romantic place, and he had a surprise for me.

*

WELL, THE BEST WAY To keep a low profile is to get yourself lost in a crowd, so I took a bus to Market Street 'cause they was havin' the Gay Pride Parade. I also set my phone so I could speed-dial Agent Jackson 'cause Agent Jackson said to call him quick if I got into trouble.

When I got off the bus at Market Street, the parade was already starting, so I found me a spot on the sidewalk where I could get myself a good view. While I was watching them women on motorbikes and them colorful marching bands, I wondered how come being gay meant ya got to have a parade. Shucks, that weren't like winning the ping-pong championship of Chinatown— it weren't even like coming in second 'cause ya lost by a coupla points. But I gotta admit that some of them marchers were really kinda amusing. There was guys wearing wigs and party dresses just like Warden Jordan, and there was people dressed up in horse costumes and pulling carts along. And then I saw this float with a sign that said Leather Pride, and the float was filled with men wearing nothin' but loin straps made outta leather. And them fellas was dancing around on the float and tickling each other with whips, and one of them fellas noticed me and let out a giant whoop. "Yo, yo, yo!" he shouted. "It's Little Miss Twinkle Toes!" And that fella he hopped right offa the float and grabbed me by the wrist. "Whaddya doin' just watching?" he asked. "You belong on a fetish float."

That fella he hoisted me onto the float and he asked me to wave at the crowd, and I heard some people cryin' out, "Hey, it's Little Miss Twinkle Toes." And I saw a local news crew following us and aiming a camera at me, and the fella who grabbed me yanked off my sandals and asked me to walk on his chest.

Now, I ain't gonna say it weren't kinda fun to be standing on that float, but when it came to keeping a low profile, I weren't doin' a very good job.

*

WELL, THAT FLOAT it inched down Market Street as slow as a slug on a rug. That's 'cause men kept crowding around it and taking photos of me with their cell phones. And one of 'em reached up and handed me a box of flavored condoms, and he slapped a ballpoint pen into my hand and asked me to sign the box.

After an hour, I felt as trapped as a cricket in a Mason jar. Shucks, even more fellas was packed around the float shouting, "Hey, Miss Twinkle Toes," and a coupla policemen in riot gear were trying to push 'em away. And when some wiry dude wearing a horse head mask pulled himself onto the stage, I speed-dialed Agent Jackson 'cause I suspected things was gonna get worse. That fella was snorting like a gut-shot stag and waving a pair of handcuffs and, next thing I knew, he grabbed me and cuffed my hands behind my back. And if that weren't insulting enough, the dude lifted me onto his shoulders then he jumped off the float and trotted towards Beale Street, touting me on his back. And the guys on the float were clapping like seals and singing some song called "Macho Man." I guess they thought that creepy fella was putting on some kinda skit.

Well, the dude carried me into a parking garage—he was stronger than a colt. And he shoved me into the front of a minivan that had a busted taillight. The van also had a license plate that said Pay Less Car Rental. When he slipped behind the steering wheel and pulled off his horse head mask, I saw that he was a real young fella who had a beetle-brow.

The fella stuck the key into the ignition and the van gave a hollow growl, then the dude he started stammering like he'd just woke up a bear. "I 'pologize for the n-noise," he said, "but ya w-won't have to hear it for long."

The dude had a Kentucky accent, but that weren't no comfort at all. I felt like a hive of yellow jackets were humming around my head.

"How long 'til I don't gotta hear it?" I said. "Are you the Muffler Man?"

The dude reached under his seat and pulled out a nine millimeter Glock, and the gun had a tube attached to the barrel that looked like a silencer. "Sorry 'bout the n-noise," he said, "but ya won't have to h-hear it for long."

The fella ripped outta the parking space, smashing into a parked sedan, then he peeled towards the exit without leaving its driver no note. And while he drove, he kept that pistol tucked under one of his legs, and his hands hung onto the steering wheel as though he was clutchin' a snake.

Well, the fella turned south on Third Street and we headed towards Hunter's Point, and all the time he kept apologizing for the racket the car was making. He said he hit a patch of construction that busted up the muffler, and he didn't have time to mess with no insurance forms. And then the dude started explaining why he was bumping me off. He said the Sugar Shack cartel had recruited him to deliver some dresses, and now he hadda do hit to prove he weren't no snitch. He said it weren't nothing personal but wanted to hang onto his life—he didn't wanna end up like Juan Perez who hadda shoot himself in the head.

Well, dern, if that fella didn't keep jabbering all the way to Hunter's Point, and when we turned into John McLaren Park he kept on jacking his jaws. He said he never snuffed out nothin' before but a cat that raided his henhouse—he said he stuffed that cat into a burlap bag and tossed it into a crik. He said he hoped he weren't going to hell for drowning that feral cat, but if that was the case, it wouldn't make no difference if he knocked off a person too.

The fella told me that someday soon he was gonna mend his ways. He was gonna get himself baptized and give his life to Lord. Well, believe it or not, I felt kinda mean when I didn't say "Hallelujah!" I felt the same way I did when I shooed them pigs outta the church.

*

AS WE DROVE through John McLaren Park, it surprised me how ordinary things looked. There was gangs of kids playing soccer, there was dogs chasing tennis balls, there was families sitting at picnic tables and cooking on barbeque grills. And the fella who had kidnapped me seemed awful ordinary too. He said he used to raise pit bulls, and his name was Cecil Dobbs.

It weren't 'til the fella parked by some woods that I lost control of my bladder. He parked on an empty road that was overlooking a pond, and that's when my bladder warmed my thighs like it had a mind of its own. And Cecil Dobbs said he was sorry I stank up my pretty dress. He said he'd have stopped at a privy if he knew I needed to pee.

We sat in the van for a coupla minutes while Cecil talked about mending his ways, then he racked the slide of his handgun and said it was time to go. He said we was going into the woods, and he asked if I wouldn't mind walking. He said he musta strained his back when was carrying me.

Well, there weren't no point in hollering out 'cause there was nobody around to hear me. And I didn't wanna leave no pee-stained corpse where anyone could find it. So I scooted outta the van when Cecil opened the passenger door. Cecil asked me to walk in front of him 'cause I sobbin' like a tot. He said it was way too hard on his nerves to deal with a woman's tears.

We walked for awhile, and we come to a crik then we didn't walk no more. Cecil he asked me to sit on a rock and watch the flow of the crik. "Ya d-don't have to see it comin'," he said. "That ain't how it's g-gonna work. Just sit on a rock and l-look at the crik. Maybe sing yourself a song."

Cecil he helped me sit down on a rock 'cause them handcuffs made sitting hard. And I said, if he weren't in no hurry, I'd sing us a song from *Annie*. And Cecil he told me to take my time so I started singing "Tomorrow," but I couldn't put no heart in it cause tomorrow it weren't gonna come. But Cecil he told me I sang real nice and there weren't no need to be nervous, and he said to pretend I was standing onstage and about to get an applause. So I imagined I was singing with Tommy Lee Weaver and I watched the crik roll by, then I heard a boom like a thunderclap announcing Judgement Day.

*

WELL, THERE'S THINGS I weren't expecting to happen when I took my leave from this world. I weren't expecting my skin to prickle like ants were gobbling me up, and I weren't expecting the stink of sulfur to linger in the air. So I figgered I was burning in hell 'cause I didn't deserve nothin' better. I guess that was bound to happen because of my decadent ways.

Someone was standing behind me and he yanked me to my feet, and he freed me from them handcuffs 'cause there ain't no escapin' from hell. And hell didn't look no different from John McLaren Park, and the person standing behind me spoke and he sounded like Agent Jackson. "Gertie, don't turn around!" he said, and his voice had the sting of a whip. "Keep your eyes on the creek. Don't look at the body. I blew away half of his head."

Agent Jackson put his jacket over my shoulders and he led me out of the woods, and I could see lotsa cops running about and stretching yellow tape 'round the trees. Well, I decided I weren't in hell even though I'd led me a sinful life, but it weren't much consolation to be wearing a pee-soaked dress. I was blushing like a ripe tomato, my stomach was fulla knots, and I felt like goblins would snatch me if I didn't wash the dress quick. But Agent Jackson he didn't say nothin' 'bout my sopping dress. He just muttered into a two-way radio and clutched my arm as we walked.

While we was sitting in the front of a squad car, Agent Jackson told me what just happened, and his voice got all shrunk up and shaky like a candle flame caught in a draft. "Lordy," he said to me.

90

"Wow, wow, wow. I had that boy in my pistol sites and I told him to lay down his rod, but instead he pointed it right at my chest like he was going to take me out. But then he froze up like a statue, and I blew off half of his head."

Agent Jackson kept talking, and I turned my eyes away. I didn't want him to put up with a woman's tears like Cecil Dobbs hadda do. And I hoped Cecil Dobbs weren't kept outta heaven 'cause of all the mischief he done. Shucks, that boy he never killed nothin' but some lowdown, egg-stealin' cat.

"Howja know where to find me?" I said.

Agent Jackson he stroked my neck, and his hand was trembling bad. He said, "John McLaren Park is where the bodies are dumped. It was pretty much a no-brainer that I would find you here."

"Howja know I'd been kidnapped?" I asked 'cause I felt mighty puzzled 'bout that. It was kinda like tryin' to figger out if pigs belong in a church.

Agent Jackson took my hand like he was picking up a kitten. And he spoke to me so tender that I felt like a newborn pup. He said the boy that kidnapped me weren't no professional killer. He said it weren't hard to know I'd been nabbed 'cause it was televised on the local news.

*

WELL, THERE AIN'T TOO MUCH LEFT to this story, and my life has improved for the better. 'Cept that I'm all the time watchin' for goblins, and I flinch when I hear a loud noise. But I don't wanna go into stuff like that 'cause it's getting me off the subject. So I'm gonna go back to what happened after Agent Jackson drove me outta the park.

I spent the night in the General Hospital so the doctors could check me out, and they let me go the next morning 'cause I'm healthier 'an a hog. And Agent Jackson he came to fetch me, and he said he had plans for us. He gave me a brand new cotton dress to replace the one I peed in, and he gave me a new pair of sandals that had comfortable rubber soles. And while we was walking outta the hospital, I slipped my hand into his, and I told him I hoped he had a good breakfast before coming to pick me up.

Well, Agent Jackson he drove me to Yerba Buena Gardens, and we sat among all them flower beds overlooking the Martin Luther King Fountain. And he told me that he'd loved me from the moment he put me in handcuffs, and he said that he would be grateful if I would consider becoming his wife.

Well, an offer like that don't need pondering at all, and I gave Agent Jackson a hug. I told him I'd be honored to accept his proposal, but I hoped he weren't expecting no lady. I said it was really considerate of him to overlook my perverted ways.

We got wed a few days later in San Francisco City Hall. That was where Marilyn Monroe married Joe DiMaggio 'bout a hundred years ago. We only had a coupla guests and my folks they couldn't come, but the Nose flew up from Los Angeles to stand in for my father. And, all the time I was saying my vows, the Nose wept like a broken pump. He said the privilege of giving me away was the proudest moment of his life.

After Agent Jackson and I tied the knot, I asked him 'bout Warden Jordan. I said maybe I shoulda let bygones be bygones and invited him to the wedding. Agent Jackson he told me that Warden Jordan had a more pressing engagement. He said that Warden Jordan was under arrest and in federal custody, 'cause he told that Sugar Shack cartel I was living in San Francisco. Agent Jackson said the warden was probably bound for the Allenwood Correctional Facility, but it might not be too hard on him 'cause they play lotsa ping-pong there.

*

THAT'S 'BOUT ALL I GOT TO SAY 'cept that I'm back in Kentucky now. I'm living in a bungalow home in Louisville, overlooking the Ohio River. The house ain't far from Frankfort Avenue where there's lotsa coffee shops, and I visit the coffee shops all the time 'cause Agent Jackson ain't home too much. I also play a whole lotta ping-pong at a nearby YMCA.

When he's home, Agent Jackson gets drunk 'cause his nerves are pretty shot, and sometimes I gotta take his arm and help him get into bed. Agent Jackson says I'm his champion and he can always depend on me, and I tell him I'll always stand by his side 'cause I'm just that kinda girl. But there's times late at night when I can't sleep too well 'cause he's snoring like a troll. And I get to thinking 'bout goblins and I look for 'em under the bed, and I even check the closets to make sure there ain't nothin' there. Ma she got it right when she read that poem to me. There's goblins sure to getcha if ya don't watch out.

8. Armadillo Slick

IT'S ME AGAIN, Gertie McDowell. It's been a while since I told you stuff, and I apologize for that. Since Agent Jackson passed last year, I've been doing rather poorly. Agent Jackson had him some liver trouble and he turned as yellow as pus, and he passed away in a hospital bed while I was lying beside him. When I phoned the Nose and told him that Agent Jackson had passed, the Nose had the sand to ask me if the bottle done him in. I guess the Nose knew that Agent Jackson had a likker habit, but that got me riled 'cause the Nose shoulda known that you oughta respect the dead. So I told him a man like Agent Jackson would never drink himself to death. I told him what Agent Jackson died of was cirrhosis of the liver.

The time's been crawlin' as slow as a snail since Agent Jackson passed, but last month I managed to turn twenty-three, and Ma she wrote me a letter. She wrote, *Gertie, you're a woman now, so it's time you were showing some sense. It's time you stopped posing on porn sites and selling illegal drugs, and it's time you stopped consorting with perverts and common drunks. You had best put your trust in the Lord from now on and build up some treasure in heaven.* And then she went on to assure me how I been heading for hell, and how I'll be sittin' on blisterin' coals if I didn't correct my ways.

Well, that ain't no advice to give a girl who's lost the love of her life. If the Lord had struck me with measles, I'd have been okay with that, but when he took away Agent Jackson, He charged me too much for my sins. The way I'm starting to look at it is that I got some more sin coming.

I ain't in Witness Protection no more—I got pulled outta that. Some clerk from the Justice Department called me and said I weren't never a witness. He said I didn't qualify for protection, but that didn't bother me none. It means I don't gotta check with the feds every time I gotta pee.

So I'm living in South Texas now on a ranch near the Rio Grande. The ranch belongs to Bertha Jean—she's outta prison now, and after Agent Jackson passed, she invited me to come stay with her. Well, I needed a change of scenery, so I accepted her invitation 'cause Kentucky ain't no place to be when you're already feeling depressed. But a change of scenery don't do that much to ease a heart that's still bleeding. Especially when the scenery ain't nothin' but cactuses and chaparral flats.

Bertha Jean and I live alone on the ranch 'cept for a few longhorn strays and some chickens. The ranch used to belong to her pa, but her pa ain't with her no more. Her pa got stuck by a mesquite thorn and his blood got poisoned bad, and he willed the ranch to Bertha Jean before he passed away. Bertha Jean wishes he'd willed her a Lexus SUV instead. She says she ain't got no use for the ranch 'cause she don't like doin' chores. Bertha Jean spends her time writing stories though she ain't published none of 'em yet.

The ranch ain't too far from the town of Laredo, which has a song named after it. When I get to feeling restless, I drive Bertha Jean's pickup into town, and I ride this mechanical bull in a bar called Cherokee Sal's. Bertha Jean ain't allowed in the bar—she got a stay-away order from it—but I'm always welcome there 'cause I ride the bull real good. They call me Bronco Betsy since I hardly never get thrown, and the bar lets customers work the controls, so they can try to toss me off. There's a sign in front of the bull that says, *Unseat Bronco Betsy,* and a waitress will serve a steak with trimmings to anyone who manages to throw me.

Now if a customer working the controls looks kinda down on his luck, I'll let myself slip off the bull so he can have him a free dinner, but most of the time I stick to the bull like I been superglued to its hide. I gotta say this 'bout the bull, it's pretty good for depression. Shucks, you can't be dwelling on no broken heart when you're riding a robot bull, so there's nights I'll ride that contraption maybe twenty or thirty times. I guess I don't care about nothin' as much as I do that mechanical bull.

*

SOMETIMES I SIT on the veranda along with Bertha Jean, and we keep an eye out for wetbacks as we watch the sun go down. And sometimes I open the Bible to seek some comfort there, but the Bible don't help me nearly as much as that doggone mechanical bull. Heck, the only verse that makes sense to me now is the one about Doubting Thomas. You can only read about Doubting Thomas in the Gospel According to John, 'cause Thomas he were a skeptic so he ain't too popular. When the other disciples told Thomas that Jesus had rose from the dead, Thomas said he wouldn't believe that unless he saw Jesus' wounds. Well, Jesus came back a second time just to show Doubting Thomas his scars, and Jesus weren't happy with Thomas 'cause he didn't have no blind faith.

Well, Doubting Thomas he had a point, and I told that to Bertha Jean. I told her I prayed my heart out when Agent Jackson was dying, but a buncha nothing is all I got for trusting in the Lord. I told her a buncha nothing weren't helpful to me at all, and if I hadda pick between nothing and grief I'd just as soon settle for grief. Bertha Jean said the course of true love is *bound* to end in grief, and that's why she weren't allowed to go into Cherokee Sal's. Bertha Jean said she was hoping one day to have a respectable love, but that the love of her life is a beer-serving woman in a rundown, honkytonk bar. She was talking 'bout Brandi Fay who is one of the waitresses there. She's a skinny young woman who wiggles her butt, so's to get herself bigger tips. Bertha Jean said that Brandi Fay's father made her file that stay-away order. That's 'cause he's too fulla religion to approve of two women in love.

"The heart wants what it wants," said Bertha Jean, and she sighed like a dog in a pound. That expression is real familiar to me—I saw it in *The Hollywood Reporter*. Woody Allen he said that when he married his Korean stepdaughter.

*

WELL, WE WAS SITTIN' ON the veranda and we was watchin' the sun go down, and Bertha Jean gave me a letter to take to Brandi Fay. She didn't put her name on the letter, she just signed it *An Admirer*. She said Brandi Fay's father is as mean as a pit bull and beats Brandi Fay when she strays, and he tells her that God made Adam and Eve—He didn't make Eve and Abby. She said if he knew that Brandi Fay was getting correspondence from her, he would probably hogtie Brandi Fay then lock her in a shed. Bertha Jean said she feels real bad about putting her lover at risk, but if bliss was their destination, it was only a sin away.

Well, I told you I got some sin comin' to me, so I said I'd deliver the letter. 'Cause I owe a lot more to Bertha Jean than I do to the word of the Lord. Shucks, Bertha Jean she *listens* to me when I talk about my troubles, and she gave away tampons when we was in prison so I could get my hair done. Maybe I oughta mend my ways so's to build up treasure in heaven, but I think I'd be a lot happier in hell if I helped out Bertha Jean.

When there weren't much sunset left to watch, I hopped into Bertha Jean's pickup, and I drove the truck to Laredo so's to give Brandi Fay the letter. And when I noticed the tumbleweeds crossing the road and the buzzards soaring above me, I got to thinking 'bout that song that's called "The Streets of Laredo." It's a song about a dying cowboy who keeps sayin' that he done wrong. The cowboy is all repentant and he's whiter 'an a sheet, and he asks that someone bang the drum slowly while he's getting put in the ground. But the song don't bother to mention what wrong that cowboy done. Shucks, he might have just peed on the sidewalk or shot him an egg-stealin' dog.

Well, I parked the truck and went into the bar, and Brandi Fay she was there. She was flirting with a coupla cowhands who looked like they were drunk, and them cowhands were too dumb to realize she was buttering them up for tips. Heck, one of 'em grabbed Brandi Fay by the arm and tried to give her a kiss, and Brandi Fay she slipped out of his grip like a lizard shedding its tail. Brandi Fay ain't that purty—she got a nose like a hawk—but she got a manner about her that's really sociable. I never seen no one half as sociable as Brandi Fay.

Well, I handed Brandi Fay the letter and she looked at me kinda curious like maybe I was serving her a notice to appear in court. "It's from an admirer," I explained and Brandi Fay she laughed. She got a laugh like a slot machine that's spilling out silver dollars.

"Honey," said Brandi Fay, "that doesn't narrow it down."

Well, I couldn't say nothin' more 'bout the letter, so I asked Brandi Fay a question. I asked her if Doubting Thomas had a point when he questioned the Resurrection.

"Hon," said Brandi Fay, "I'm a waitress in a dive. If I believed in resurrections, do you think I'd be here serving drunks?"

I guess Brandi Fay had a point as well, so I asked her another question. I asked her if she knew what that cowboy done wrong in that song called "The Streets of Laredo."

"Dunno," said Brandi Fay with a wink. "He probably short-changed a waitress. Hey, why don't you get your buns back on that bull and stop asking me silly questions?"

*

I WISH EVERYTHING came as easy to me as riding that mechanical bull. Ya just gotta shift your butt cheeks when you feel the bull starting to turn, and you just gotta hold out your riding hand in the opposite direction. But when you're messing around with affairs of the heart, there ain't no girth to hang onto, and I started feeling the way I felt when I dreamed about the Muffler Man. I felt that something real uncommon was sizing me up again, so I weren't surprised when I saw this strange fella working the controls of the bull.

The fella he looked like nobody that I ever seen before. He looked 'bout as tall as a grandfather clock even though he was sitting down, and his face was as cracked as an ol' red barn that had been in a hundred storms. The Stetson hat he was wearing was as wide as a barrel cactus, and his jeans were so bleached from the sun that they was practically white. The fella he hadda be sixty years old, but he looked as strong as an oak tree, and I ain't seen no one control the bull the way that fella was doin'. He was working the dials and the joystick like he was playing a concert piano, and whenever some dude climbed onto the bull, he got thrown in less 'an three seconds.

The fella turned and looked at me as if he been waiting for me to show up, and he spoke to me real familiar like he'd known me all my life. "I had almost givin' up waitin' for you," he said in this lazy drawl, and I felt the chill of winter go running down my spine.

"I hope you ain't here to arrest me," I said. "All I done was deliver a letter."

The fella he rose to his feet and he smelled of tobacco and whiskey, and he gazed at me like a squirrel that had spotted itself a nut. "No need to fret, lil' darlin'," he said as he tipped his Stetson hat. "Everything about you is arrestin' already, so why would I need to do that?"

He smiled at me kinda gentle like he was havin' himself some fun, and he kept looking at me like he knowed me since I was knee-high to a duck. And the more that fella looked at me, the creepier I felt. He was acting like he had purchased me from them San Francisco slavers.

"Mister," I said, "you don't need to do nothin' but tell me who you are."

The dude stroked his jaw as if my question needed some real deep thought. Like maybe he had him a secret that he weren't too inclined to share. When he finally spoke, his voice sorta flowed like water in a crik. "Darlin'," he said, "you can call me Armadillo Slick."

*

WELL, THERE WEREN'T NOBODY mounting the bull no more, so the fella and I had a chat. He told me he was a horse trader and he had a spread north of Laredo, and it got pretty lonesome on the range and that suited him just fine. But he said that now an' then he got him an itch for some female company, and when he got that itch, he drove into town and roped him a local filly. He said there weren't no place better 'an Cherokee Sal's for curing him of his itch.

Now that fella seemed kinda knowledgeable, so I asked him about that cowboy song. I asked if he knowed what that cowboy done wrong to get himself put in the ground.

The fella he filled a shot glass with whiskey and he contemplated the question, then he said, "Ya don't gotta do nothing wrong to get yourself put in the ground. The only thing doin' wrong might do is speed it up a bit."

I said, "I'll bet that cowboy did nothing but shoot him a thievin' dog."

The dude took him a sip of whiskey and swished it around in his mouth. "Say, lil' darlin," he said, after swallowin' the whiskey, "how come I get the impression that you've been tempting fate?"

Dern, it was like that fella could see right into my soul. When I said all I done was deliver a letter, he said, "That ain't the point. Folks are callin' you Bronco Betsy. You're famous in most of the county. Don't you know sooner or later you're gonna get thrown from that bull?"

"Shucks," I said, "I seen *Urban Cowboy* six or seven times. John Travolta tempted fate much worse 'an me, and he didn't get thrown at all. He rode out that bull in Gilley's Bar and won himself a contest."

The dude opened a pouch of Redman Tobacco and he tucked a chaw under his cheek, and he said, "You ain't never rode a bull controlled by Armadillo Slick. If you can last the full eight seconds when it's *my* hand on the joystick, I'll eat a red hot pepper and take you out to dinner."

Well, I didn't say nothin' more to him, I just climbed up on the bull. And the bull started twirling and jerking so fast it was like I was in a tornado. The room weren't nothin' but a blur, my head snapped like a whip, and the girth bit into my fingers like it had a set of teeth. But I lasted the full eight seconds and folks in the bar started clapping, and that dude hung his head like a scalded dog when he switched off the controls.

"'Darlin'," he said, "you just got the best of Armadillo Slick. Let's find an Outback Steakhouse because I'm takin' you out to dine."

*

I'M GONNA CHANGE the subject for a moment 'cause I remember something Ma told me. She said a woman has just one true love, and it's all downhill after that. She said the love of her life weren't Pa even though they was wed for twenty-five years. She said the fella that captured her heart was a dude that cleaned out porta-potties. She met him at a bluegrass festival when she was only sixteen, and they had 'em a torrid affair that only lasted a week. She said the fella left her to marry his high school sweetheart, and her heart went to sleep after that and never woke up again. She said no one ever rang her chimes like that porta-potty fella.

While I was sittin' in that Outback Steakhouse with Armadillo Slick, I remembered Ma telling me that, and my heart broke all over again. So I told him I was a widder and I weren't in no market for sex, and I weren't gonna love nobody ever again like I loved Agent Jackson.

Armadillo Slick he was dipping cheese fries into a cheddar and bacon dip, and he said that didn't bother him none 'cause them cheese fries were as good as sex. And he said a blooming onion was even better 'an sex, provided that you ordered it with two cups of spicy sauce. "Anyhow," he said, "once I've mounted a filly, I like to dump her fast. I ain't sure I'm in that big a hurry to get myself shed of you."

Well, I suppose the dude was having himself some fun at my expense. But he seemed to be kinda friendly and he weren't too hard to talk to, and I wanted a second opinion about what I was doin' for Bertha Jean. I told him I done time in Alderson Prison and that's where I met Bertha Jean, and Bertha Jean gave some tampons away so I could get my hair done. I said I was beholdin' to Bertha Jean 'cause my hair got fixed real nice, so I was helping Bertha Jean hook up with a woman she weren't allowed to see.

Armadillo Slick told me he knew Bertha Jean since she was a teenager stealing from pharmacies, and he knew Bertha Jean been to prison for soliciting bogus donations. He said he weren't aware that she was out of the pokey now, and he didn't know that she'd found herself a friend as good as me. "Ain't it amazin'," he said, "what a handful of tampons will fetch?"

I gotta say this 'bout Armadillo Slick—he sure could make me laugh.

*

ARMADILLO SLICK kept sipping whiskey while we was eating them Outback steaks, and the likker musta primed his tongue 'cause he told me some more about him. He told me he was a fifth-generation Texan, the kind who likes open ranges, but one day he married a Kickapoo whore he met in a Dallas brothel. He said that was a damn fool thing to do 'cause he weren't sober at the time, and women get pricklier 'an grass spurs if ya let 'em hang around. But at least that whore had the decency to run off with a veterinarian, and she left him a note that said she weren't suited to his all his ramblin' ways. He said that nothin' came of that marriage but a blazing dose of the clap and a daughter he ain't seen for thirty years 'cause she's a church-goin' type of person.

"Didja make her stay home and slop a hog?" I asked Armadillo Slick. "I ain't gonna fault your daughter none if ya had her sloppin' a hog."

Armadillo Slick he laughed and said, "We ain't here to talk about hogs. We're here so I can tell you how to ride a robot bull proper." Well, he took another a slug of whiskey and he ate the last bite of his steak, then he said, "Darlin', when you're ridin' one of them bulls, you don't wanna hang on every time. The only time you wanna stay on it is once the odds against you are high."

He went on to explain that there's bull ridin' contests in bars all over Texas, and that there's bookies laying odds as to who's gonna win them contests. The trick, he said, is to fall off the bull when they're having the practice rounds, and to hang onto the bull for the full eight seconds after the odds against you are set. "That's how you bring home the bacon," he said, "without havin' to slop no hog."

*

WELL, THAT'S HOW THINGS got started between me and Armadillo Slick. He entered me in bull riding contests in bars all over Texas, and the time it didn't drag so much when we was on the road. We entered bull riding contests in Austin and Houston and San Antonio, and I made it a point to fall off the bull quick during the practice rounds. By the time the final round began, the odds against me were steep, 'cause the folks in them cities weren't yet aware that I was Bronco Betsy. I won almost all the contests though the prize money weren't that much, but Armadillos Slick made thousands of dollars by betting with bookies and customers. We split the money fifty-fifty 'cause that's what I thought was fair. Otherwise, I think Armadillo Slick woulda let me have it all.

One time we drove all the way to Dallas where they got a bar called Gilley's. It's a spinoff of that bar near Houston where they filmed *Urban Cowboy*. I seen that movie a coupla times 'cause I really like John Travolta, but the character he played in that movie almost turned me offa him. He played this phony cowboy who was dumb as a pimpleback oyster. All the dude did was dance the two-step and knock his girlfriend around, and he couldn't even order a hamburger without throwing it at the waitress. I suppose John Travolta was playing a fella a whole lot dumber than him, but after that movie came out, I'm surprised that he kept any fans at all.

Well, at that bull riding contest at Gilley's, we got into a peck of trouble. After I won the contest and collected a five hundred dollar prize, a buncha rowdies approached us while we was in the parking lot. One of them rowdies asked me if I was Bronco Betsy 'cause he'd heard of this girl in Laredo who never got thrown off the bull. The dudes had lost a passel of cash to Armadillo Slick, and, since things didn't seem on the up-and-up to 'em, they wanted their money back.

Armadillo Slick asked them to wait while he fetched his money belt, and he reached into the cab of his pickup truck and pulled out a two-barreled shotgun. He said, "How about double or nothing, boys?" and them rowdies scattered like crows. And Armadillo Slick he emptied both barrels an inch or two over their heads.

As he drove us back to Laredo, Armadillo Slick whooped like a rustler. He said we weren't hustling Gilley's no more 'cause he don't like the company there, and he said he never had as much fun with his daughter as he was having with me.

I believe Doubtin' Thomas would have plenty of doubt about me and Armadillo Slick. 'Cause I don't suppose I was building up a speck of treasure in heaven. But treasure in heaven ain't tempting enough when you're hurting to get through the day. And the day didn't weigh so heavy when I was with Armadillo Slick.

*

AFTER WE HUSTLED Gilley's and headed back to Laredo, Armadillo Slick he kept swigging from a bottle of Johnny Walker. The pickup truck started weaving like he was driving on ice, and it would only have been a couple of seconds 'til we was wrapped around a tree. So I asked him to pull over 'cause my bladder was about to burst, and after we both had a pee, I slipped behind the steering wheel. Shucks, just 'cause my heart was broken didn't mean I was in a hurry to leave this world. It wouldn't have been no improvement to be sittin' on blistering coals.

Once we got back to Webb County, I drove us to Bertha Jean's ranch house. Armadillo Slick he needed to drink a pot of real strong coffee, and no one makes coffee stronger than Bertha Jean. It hits you like a bolt of lightning snaking outta the sky. And since we'd done enough sinning to earn us a bolt of lightning, it'd be best if it sprang from a pot of coffee and not the fist of the Lord.

There weren't no lights on in the ranch house, but I could still make out Bertha Jean. She was sitting on the veranda, watching our truck approach, and a harvest moon had lit her up like a spotlight mighta done. It looked like she weren't of this world no more and was waitin' to tell me goodbye.

Well, I sat down on a rocker beside her and a chill kinda tickled my neck, and I heard a horned owl hoo-hooing when Bertha Jean took my hand. She didn't say nothing at first, she just sat there holding my hand. And Armadillo Slick he stayed in the truck 'cause he weren't fit for nothing but sleeping.

After a while, Bertha Jean started jawing 'bout our time at Alderson Prison. She talked about how nice my hair looked after she gave them tampons away, and she talked about how I made her proud when I skunked everyone at checkers. She even talked about Warden Jordan and how he was fulla surprises, and how it was hard to know if he was speaking to you on account of his lazy eye. But it didn't seem like Bertha Jean was sharing no memories. It was like she was reading from a book that she maybe found in a bus station. And Armadillo Slick he kept snoring 'cause he weren't fit for nothin' else. He sounded like a chain saw that was cutting down a tree.

*

AFTER WE SAT on the veranda a spell, Bertha Jean changed the subject. She told me about something she said she'd been keeping inside her for a while. She said heaven was surely a sin away if she could run off with Brandi Fay, but if the sin was committed by Brandi Fay's father, things weren't gonna work out so well. She said Brandi Fay's father had served time in Huntsville for stabbing an Austin man to death, and he had knocked off several other folks for which he had never been caught. She said that folks called him Abraham after that fella in the Bible—that's 'cause he's all the time quotin' scripture and wielding a knife for the Lord. She said he visited her last Sunday and his eyes were fulla fire, and he was carrying the letter I delivered to Brandi Fay. And he told her that it weren't proper of her not to sign the letter, 'cause the letter was her death certificate and her name oughta be on that.

When Bertha Jean told him the Bible only gave him the right to kill beasts, he said women that fornicate with each other ain't no better 'an beasts. He said he weren't gonna kill her on a Sunday 'cause the Sabbath belongs to the Lord, but he was gonna come back in a coupla days and put her in the ground.

Well, the moon was as bright as a headlight and that owl was as loud as a horn, and I realized how much them tampons were gonna cost me now. There weren't no doubt in my mind about what Bertha Jean wanted me to do. 'Cause Bertha Jean she's a felon and felons ain't allowed to do much. They're only allowed to get carved up by fellas that folks call Abraham.

Ya know, sin is as cheap as a dime-store ring when you've committed a passel of them. 'Cause untangling a pack of transgressions is harder than committing yourself one more. So I took some comfort in knowing that I was heading straight to hell, and that them coals wouldn't burn no hotter if I bought Bertha Jean a gun.

I GOTTA TELL YA about this dream I had after talking with Bertha Jean. I ain't sure why I gotta call it a dream 'cause it was as real as a bellyache. But when something don't lend itself to explaining and sorta shakes you up, people ain't gonna be comfortable unless you call it a dream. So I'm gonna say I was dreaming 'cause I gotta finish this story.

The dream it happened in Bertha Jean's guestroom, which weren't fit for no visitations. There weren't nothing in that guestroom but a cot and a broken-back rocker, and my clothes were strewn all over the floor 'cause I had no place to store 'em. Well, I felt a breeze tickling my forehead as I was drifting off to sleep, and when I opened my eyes, I saw Agent Jackson sitting in that broken-back rocker. He was sitting there quiet as a lizard and he was reading a newspaper, and he was flipping through the pages like he was hoping the news would change.

"How are you doing, Gertie?" he said, and he kept on turning pages. He was probably real uncomfortable to be haunting so messy a room.

Well, I guess he needed to hear a lie, so I said I was doin' well. And when he didn't respond, I knew that the talking was gonna be up to me. So I told him I was keeping company with a fella named Armadillo Slick, but that I weren't gonna have no sex with him 'cause we'd rather eat blooming onions. I said I never liked onions much, but they taste real good when they're blooming, and then I asked him how heaven was 'cause I wanted to be polite.

Agent Jackson he didn't say nothin' for what seemed like a real long time. He just kept reading the newspaper and glancing out the window, and I weren't sure he had even heard me' 'til he finally cleared his throat. "It's sort of like San Francisco here," he said, and he turned another page. "I always liked San Francisco, Gertie. Except for the traffic and bums."

I told him I liked San Francisco too, especially Golden Gate Park, and I liked when we sat by that big ol' pond and watched them geese eating bugs.

"Did we?" he said, and he rattled the newspaper. "Things kind of get away from you here."

Well, I ain't sure why Agent Jackson had come to pay me a visit. Even when he spoke, he never looked in my direction. But that was probably for the best 'cause my face was scalded with tears, and Agent Jackson seemed troubled enough without seeing no woman's tears.

As I looked at Agent Jackson, I remembered somethin' Ma told me. She said folks in heaven might pay you a visit, but they weren't gonna hang around long. 'Cause the dead got business they gotta get on with, and that business don't include you.

But I sensed that trouble was coming my way and it felt like it was close, and I sensed that Agent Jackson knew that too, but weren't allowed to do nothin' about it. I don't think that Agent Jackson was pleased that he hadda get back to heaven. I don't think heaven was meant for a manly fella like him.

After a while, he pushed himself out of the chair and came over to where I was lying, and he stroked my head with his palm, which felt as chilled as a channel catfish. And that rocker it swayed like a pendulum while he was telling me goodbye. He told me he'd love me forever, and he kissed me on the forehead. And his breath it smelled like ashes that was cooling in a stove.

*

WHEN I WOKE the next morning, I wondered why I hadn't heard Bertha Jean's rooster. She has this bantam rooster that's been waking us up at sunrise, and she says she'd like to wring his neck, but she needs him to breed with the hens. So I got outta bed and went out on the porch, and I noticed the sun was high. And I saw this big ol' javelina gobblin' that rooster up.

I didn't see Bertha Jean nowhere and her pickup truck was gone, and Armadillo Slick he was sitting on the porch all by himself. His feet was propped up on the railing and his hat was shading his eyes, and he was sipping a cup of coffee and watching that rooster get et.

When I let him know that Agent Jackson came to me in a dream, Armadillo Slick blowed on his coffee and had himself a stretch. He said he don't put no stock in dreams 'cause there's other things needing attention. He said one of them was for me to learn the right way to fall off a bull.

"Darlin'," he said, "when you're ridin' for money ya can't be too obvious. If folks think you're tryin' to fool 'em during the practice round, the odds on you will go way down and we won't be makin' no money. Ya gotta hang on a few seconds longer, so folks won't start gettin' suspicious."

He said we was goin' to Cherokee Sal's so I could put in some practice time, and I told him I weren't goin' nowhere 'til he shot that javelina. I was real fond of that rooster, ya know—I even gave him a name. I named him Little Prince Charles 'cause he was a cocky little fella, and I weren't gonna stand there a second longer and watch Prince Charles get et.

Armadillo Slick said he couldn't do nothin' about Prince Charles getting et. He said Bertha Jean told him her story about how she been tempting fate, so he gave her the loan of his shotgun so she wouldn't get stuck with a knife. He said there's too many crazies around with murder on their minds, and them crazies don't oughta be given no chance to put folks in the ground.

"Now I ain't into christenin' roosters," he said, "but I did give that shotgun a name. I call it the Faith of Job because it gives a soul confidence. Fate ain't gonna be tempted so much when you're carrying the Faith of Job."

Well, it looked like Armadillo Slick had taken my sin off my hands. And I guess I felt beholding enough to let Prince Charles get et. So I gave him a smooch on the forehead, and we got into his truck. And we headed to Cherokee Sal's, so I could learn how to fall off a bull.

*

THE TUMBLEWEEDS were floating like ghosts as we headed down the road, and I never saw so many turkey vultures hanging in the sky. And I remembered Bertha Jean talking to me with that heavenly glow in her eyes, and how that glow weren't dimmed by the thought of some fella carrying a knife. So when we parked outside of Cherokee Sal's and I saw a police car sitting there, I figgered the Faith of Job mighta had something to do with that.

Bertha Jean was sitting in the back of the police car, and she looked like she was in a trance. And a crowd had collected around Brandi Fay who was talking to a couple of cops. And Brandi Fay was pale as a corpse and holding onto one of the cops, and she weren't acting sociable no more—she was shaking her head like a mule.

Well, I felt like a wart on a peacock when I hopped outta the truck, 'cause I didn't feel too compatible with what was goin' on. Bertha Jean didn't look as though she wanted no company, and Brandi Fay was raving like she witnessed the Resurrection. I ain't that adaptable to folks when they're raving about religion—not since I hadda chase them pigs out of the church.

"It had to be a miracle," I heard Brandi Fay telling the cops. "She pointed that shotgun right at my chest and said heaven was a sin away. And then she pulled both triggers, but the shotgun didn't go off."

"Her shotgun needs a good cleaning," a cop said to Brandi Fay. "A murder-suicide ain't gonna succeed unless you use a clean gun."

"Thank god, she's a mess," said Brandi Fay, and a chuckle came into her throat. "She got things outta order too. She should have shot herself first."

Brandi Fay started telling the cop that she hardly knew Bertha Jean. She said Bertha Jean came into the bar one day and she gave Bertha Jean a smile, then she served her a free margarita 'cause it was happy hour. And Bertha Jean said one happy hour didn't compare with eternal bliss, and she came back to the bar every day for a month and kept trying to sneak a kiss. Brandi Fay said she put a stay-away order on her 'cause she didn't want that much bliss.

When I felt a hand on my elbow, I thought it was the hand of the Lord, but it was only Armadillo Slick who was leading me back to his truck. He said Bertha Jean told him a mighty fine story and she oughta get credit for that, and that when she goes back to prison, she'll have plenty of time to write herself a best seller. When I told him that Brandi Fay's father don't deserve to be in no book, he said Brandi Fay's father passed ten years ago, so I don't gotta get worked up about that. He also said I don't gotta get worked up about witnessing no miracle, 'cause it didn't take more than a flathead screwdriver to pull the firing pins out of that shotgun.

As we pulled out of the parking lot, he patted me on the arm, and he said we was heading to the Outback Steakhouse to share a blooming onion. He said this consternation weren't nothin' a blooming onion won't fix.

*

I GOT NOTHING ELSE To tell you except that I ain't left South Texas yet. I'm hanging around with Armadillo Slick and we're still entering bull riding contests, but folks are startin' to recognize me so our hustle it ain't gonna last. And I'm still staying at Bertha Jean's ranch house 'cause her chickens have gotta be fed, but if that javelina starts lickin' his chops, them chickens ain't gonna last neither. But I still owe a favor to Bertha Jean 'cause she gave all them tampons away, and feeding her chickens is a million times better than helping her kill Brandi Fay.

I wrote Ma a letter and told her what happened 'cause I needed to clear my head. And Ma she wrote back and told me that I must have a guardian angel. Well, I suppose Ma got it right again, but I feel kinda riled about that. 'Cause them angels ain't fair as to who they protect and who they let fall through the cracks. Agent Jackson deserved some protecting, but they let darkness snatch him away. And the Nose he needed to keep his muse, and they let him get robbed of his talent. Shucks, them angels have gotta be blinder than moles and without the sense God gave a turnip. But I guess fairness got nothing to do with it, and I'll have to make do with that.

I also gotta make due with the fact that angels ain't always becoming. If one of 'em is gonna lighten my load, I'd expect him to have some wings. I'd also expect him to glow like a candle and carry himself a harp, and not to be sluggin' down whiskey all day and watchin' as roosters get et. Now I ain't no expert on saviors—I got too much sin for that. But I never thought mine would be no drunk named Armadillo Slick.

Epilogue

I WAS STILL LIVING on Bertha Jean's ranch in South Texas when James Hanna sent me a package. The package contained a draft of my book along with a note he had written. He wrote that it was a really great honor to have edited my book, and he wanted me to check it over before he sent it to his publisher.

Well, I gave the book a careful read, and it looked like he got most things right. But the book didn't have no moral, and that made me feel kinda bad. So I called James Hanna on his cell phone after I'd read the book, and I mentioned that the book didn't have no moral and that disappointed me. James Hanna said morals are for fables and not to worry about that. He said he believed folks would like the book just the way it is.

James Hanna also wanted to know what I wished to name the book. Well, I thought for a minute then suggested we call it *The Perils of Gertrude McDowell*. James Hanna he said with a name like that we would only sell three or four copies. He said it'd be better to call the book *The Ping-Pong Champion of Chinatown*. He said that was a catchier title, and it would get folks to buy the book. Well, that name didn't seem no better to me, but I told James Hanna it sounded fine. There just ain't no point in debating a fella as smart as him.

James Hanna also said he was planning a book tour that would cover thirty states. He suggested I come along with him because folks will be wantin' to meet me. Well, I thought about that for a minute or two then I told him I weren't interested. Truth is I've had enough fame already to last me a couple of lifetimes. And fame is kinda disappointing when you get to thinkin' about it. Shucks, a cool glass of lemonade on a front porch is a whole lot better than fame. But I told him I was beholdin' to him and that I hoped he sold lotsa books. As for me, I was gonna sit on the porch and watch the tumbleweeds roll.

Acknowledgements

FIRST, I WOULD LIKE to thank Antaeus and Teri Moore for helping me develop story lines for Gertie McDowell, who rapidly became one of my favorite characters. And a big thanks goes to Glenna Bloomquest who portrayed Gertie in public readings. I have dedicated this book to Antaeus, Teri, and Glenna. I am also grateful to Mary, my wife, and Catherine, my mother, for supporting me in my ambition to become a prolific writer,

I am thankful to the following members of my critique group for their many comments on the Gertie stories: Robert, Marisa, Pamela, Elizabeth, Shirley, and Teresa. The book is stronger because of them.

Again, a special thanks goes to Tory Hartmann, my publisher, friend, and chief editor. Without her, this book would not have been possible.

Thank you for reading *The Ping-Pong Champion of Chinatown*. If you enjoyed it, consider telling your friends or posting a short review on Amazon. Word of mouth is an author's best friend and much appreciated.

About James Hanna

JAMES HANNA wandered Australia for seven years before settling on a career in criminal justice. He spent twenty years as a counselor in the Indiana Department of Corrections and recently retired from the San Francisco Probation Department where he was assigned to a domestic violence and stalking unit.

James' familiarity with the criminal element has provided fodder for much of his writing. His debut novel, *The Siege*, depicts a hostage standoff in a penal facility. Rob Slavens, Top 100 Reviewer, writes: "This is the raw, gritty reality of life in prison and the best of its genre that I have ever come across."

Call Me Pomeroy, James' second novel, chronicles the madcap tales of a street musician on parole who joins Occupy Oakland and its spinoff movements in Europe. He does not join for political reasons but to get on television, attract an agent and score a million dollar recording contract. The first chapter, appearing in *Empty Sink Publishing*, was deemed Editor's Choice for that issue.

James' short stories are written in many genres, including science fantasy. His tales are published in those journals that prefer stories written in blood, stories that depict unvarnished truth over political correctness. *Red Savina Review, The Literary Review, Crack the Spine* and *Sixfold* have all published James' stories. Many of James' stories appear in his third and fourth books: *A Second, Less Capable Head and Other Rogue Stories* and *Shackles and More Gripping Tales*.

James' books received two gold medals and a bronze medal from Readers' Favorite International Awards and a silver medal from Independent Press Awards.

The Ping-Pong Champion of Chinatown is James' fifth book.